The Tsaddik of the Seven Wonders

The Tsaddik of the Seven Wonders

ISIDORE HAIBLUM

DOUBLEDAY & COMPANY, INC.

GARDEN CITY, NEW YORK

1981

For Stuart Silver,
Grand Nabob
Counsel Extraordinary
Master Kokhlefel
and his beauteous wife Elizabeth,
Enchantress Supreme
and Peerless Sweetie-Pie

All of the characters in this book
are fictitious, and any resemblance
to actual persons, living or dead,
is purely coincidental.

ISBN: 0-385-17137-4
Library of Congress Catalog Card Number 81-65663

Printed in the United States of America

Contents

Linguistic note:

The Yiddish words scattered
throughout this text read pretty
much the way they are spelled:
kh should be read as in the German:
A*ch*! For that matter, so
should *Ch*elm, nebe*ch*, and *ch*utspahdik, our
three exceptions to the *kh* rule.

Tsaddik Isaac Ben Rubin a wise and holy man, official worker of miracles, a student of time - becomes lost on a trip through time and meets Myron, an evil individual from the future.

The Tsaddik Himself: One

"*Oy vey, oy vey,*" I pulled and pulled.

"What is it? What's happened?" A murmur went up from the congregation.

"Can't you see? It's his beard; it's stuck in the door!"

"Yes, it's my beard; it's stuck in the door," I yelled. "That's it." I knew it had to be something like that.

"Ah! His beard."

"It's plain now."

"It's obvious."

"We should have seen it at once."

Together they chorused: "His beard is stuck in the door."

I stopped pulling for a moment. "Is that the best you can do?" I asked irritably.

"It's a problem," a voice said.

"A catastrophe."

"It's an *umglik.*"

"Whoever heard of such a thing?"

"What's to be done?" the congregation wailed.

There was a general shrugging of shoulders, a scratching of heads, a multitude of sighs. The usual thing.

A voice from the rear of the congregation made itself heard: "Wait!"

It was Yankel the Tailor.

All eyes turned toward him. I looked too. What else was there to do?

This Yankel was a short, nearsighted man who wore his yarmulka at a rakish angle. He tapped his forehead.

"I think I've got it," he said. "I think, maybe, I know."

"Look who's talking," someone chortled.

"From a tailor, he's become a *knower*," someone else said.

A third party put in: "If he knows so much why isn't he a Rothschild?"

A learned man began a dissertation on the meaning of the word "know."

It was interesting, so I listened too.

In due course the dissertation, as was obviously the custom here, evolved into a disputation, when a wise man—one who habitually occupied a place of honor near the coveted eastern wall—bitterly attacked the entire concept of "knowing," claiming it was an illusory, unattainable objective. Everyone took sides and vigorously expounded his own approach to the problem. A problem's a problem.

I had a few ideas of my own, but, because my beard was stuck in the door, which was on one side of the chamber, I couldn't make myself heard over the *tumel*. The whole experience was proving quite unsatisfactory.

After a while it began to get dark, and it was time to go home.

People made ready to depart—but, of course, they couldn't.

Because my beard was stuck in the door.

There was, as might be expected, general consternation. Chagrin.

"Now we'll never get out," one of the wise men lamented.

"We're doomed," the fat, bearded dairyman cried out.

"It's a lost cause!" someone wailed.

Just then the little tailor pushed his way through the crowd.

"Wait!"

"So what else is there to do, with his beard stuck in the door?"

"Oh, here's the *khokhem* again."

"Advice is cheap."

"With advice, you can buy an empty egg shell."

"Listen," the little tailor said, "I *think* I have a plan. . . ."

"*Nu?*"

"Let's hear it, already."

"So what's this so-called plan?"

The tailor surveyed the crowd and said in a trembling voice: "*Maybe we should open the door?*"

They did, and the scene changed.

We were walking along on a wide, seemingly endless desert. It stretched in all directions. The sun was directly overhead. It was hot—too hot. Fortunately, I was clad in only a loincloth. Sand sifted through my toes. Hot, burning sand. Quite understandable. If it had been ice cold, under the circumstances, we'd have been in trouble. Far ahead of us, a little to the left in a shimmering haze of heat, a structure of some kind was barely discernible. We trudged toward it.

"We" was Greenberg and I.

Greenberg wasn't actually doing the walking, you understand. He usually left that to me.

Greenberg was only eight inches tall and invisible to most people. Myself excluded, of course.

Greenberg was Greenberg the Homunculus, who sat on my right shoulder.

"Greenberg," I said. "We're still in the same line?"

"Sure," Greenberg said. "Where else?"

"You're positive?" I was concerned.

"We've gone back a bit," Greenberg said. "But it's still the same line."

"This is *some* desert."

"Sure it's some desert. It's the *best* desert; they don't come any better than this, believe me."

"So why is it we're out here in the middle of nowhere?"

"What nowhere? We're going over there where that building is. See? We just missed the mark a little bit. You shouldn't worry so much. Remember, Greenberg's on the job."

Greenberg was dressed in a checkered suit. He wore a bow tie, a bowler hat and carried a bamboo cane. His shoes were white. Long ago he used to wear a toga and sandals, but no more. Greenberg has gone modern with the rest of us.

I said: "Greenberg, what was the name of that place back there?"

"*Chelm.*"

"And it's on the main line?"

"Why shouldn't it be?"

"Greenberg, if I am correct we were somehow part of that picture back there in that place."

"Chelm. Yes, I noticed that."

"And we were stuck."

"What stuck? Why make trouble and maybe start an argument? 'Delayed' would be putting it better."

I said: "Who wants to be part of a picture like that?"

"It didn't take long. It was short."

"Greenberg, I was one of the main actors!"

"I thought that little fellow, that tailor, was pretty good."

"How did that happen, Greenberg?"

"How did it happen?"

"How?"

"That's what you want to know?"

"Yes."

Greenberg nodded. "I don't know," he said.

We walked on in silence. The structure up ahead was getting bigger. There was considerable activity around it.

"Maybe it won't happen again," Greenberg said.

"Some homunculus," I said.

"Look," Greenberg said. "Do I look like a magician or something? Do you think I'm in the sorcery business? That's not my line. That's *your* line."

"Wonder-worker," I said. "Not a magician. Thurston was a magician. Blackstone was a magician. Judah the Pious was a magician."

"He wasn't so pious," Greenberg said.

"But he was a magician. I'm a wonder-worker."

"So why didn't you work a wonder back there and get us out of Chelm if you didn't like it?"

"Greenberg, I couldn't do it. I was part of the picture. That's what I've been trying to tell you."

Greenberg shook his head. "A bad precedent," he said.

"Where were you, Greenberg, when all this was going on?" I asked.

"I was dozing."

"So now my shoulder is a rest home for tired midgets."

"Homunculus. Midgets are bigger."

"Midgets are people!" I said.

"There's no need to be insulting. Look," Greenberg said, "I'll think of something."

By this time we were close enough to the structure to see what was going on.

"Look at that," I said.

Even Greenberg was impressed. "It's a temple," Greenberg told me. "When it's finished it's going to be the biggest temple the world has ever seen."

"What's it called?"

"The Temple of Amūn."

"And we are—?"

"At *El Karnak*."

"Greenberg, in Egypt?"

"Think of it—Egypt, where our people were slaves."

"*Our* people? I'm thinking of it. You couldn't have found a more cheerful place?"

"Chelm was cheerful."

"Very funny, Greenberg."

Greenberg said: "Watch out that you shouldn't step on

nothing. Everything here is sacred. That lake, see? That's sacred. Over there to the left—that building is where the war god Montu lives. That's his temple, inside there. You don't want to mess with him—"

We were close enough now to observe the individuals scurrying about. Most were clad in loincloths, brown net-like affairs made of slit leather. These persons were obviously engaged in making bricks. Even I could tell that. There were bricks everywhere, piles of bricks already hardened and rows of bricks spread out on the ground to dry. The bricks were considerably larger than those we had back in the *shtetl*. And they were gray.

"They're gray," I said.

"That's because they don't feed them good. They're slaves."

"The bricks," I said.

"Oh. Sure. That's Nile alluvium they make 'em from. Dark gray. They mix in sand or chopped barley straw as a kind of binder, see? What they're building right here is this construction ramp. They'll use it to work on the temple."

"Where did you get all this?"

"*The Encyclopaedia Britannica.* Where else? Look. Some of those guys down there by the ramp are our *landslite.*"

"*Nebech,*" I said. They didn't look very happy. Slaves, after all. "Is Moses around somewhere?"

Greenberg shook his head. "He comes later."

We were right in the center of things now. There were rows of trees. The temples, towering structures—really impressive—were built almost entirely of sandstone. They were covered with painted reliefs, pictures. Not very life-like, if you ask me. The water of the Nile was visible a little way off. It wasn't my habit to study up on these matters, of course, the way Greenberg did, but I prided myself on *some* basic knowledge.

"Smell that air," Greenberg said. "No air pollution like that other place, if you'll pardon me."

"I'm not responsible for that other place," I reminded him.

A man stepped out from behind the large mound of bricks I was leaning against. He carried a briefcase, was dressed in a gray business suit and wore a homburg hat. He tipped his hat respectfully and beamed at me. "Good afternoon," he said.

"Whatever it is, we ain't buying," Greenberg said.

The man ignored him. "My name is Myron," he grinned. He was a big fellow with an athletic build, a rosy complexion and yellow hair. "And you," he said, alluding to me, "are Issac ben Rubin the *Tsaddik*."

"Just call me Tsaddik," I said. "Everyone does." To Greenberg I said, "See? It's not the main line. This probably isn't even Egypt."

"You think I don't know my business?" Greenberg asked. "*This* is the main line."

"You'll forgive me," the man called Myron smiled. "I couldn't help overhearing what your little friend just said about that 'other place.'"

"I'm not his little friend," Greenberg said, "I'm Greenberg the Homunculus."

"Of course you are," Myron said. "Now I have just the thing here to take care of that naughty other place."

"I haven't got anything against that other place. It's Greenberg, here, who doesn't like it. See, Greenberg, this isn't the main line. Why don't you admit you've made a mistake? When *I* make a mistake, I admit it right away."

"What mistake? Where mistake? This is Greenberg you're talking to; Greenberg don't make mistakes."

Myron said: "Think of the air pollution there. It's simply terrible. Absolutely disgusting."

"Yes," I said, trying to keep from laughing, it was so obvious that we'd skipped the main line, "but that can't be helped."

"Oh! But you're wrong."

"Watch how you talk to the Tsaddik," Greenberg said.

"Quiet, Greenberg," I said.

"You can drop a hydrogen bomb on them," Myron said.

"How would that help the air pollution?" I wanted to know.

"It would fix them. They'd think twice before polluting the air again."

"They wouldn't think at all; they'd be dead," Greenberg said.

"This is a very peculiar line we're on," I said.

"Naturally," Myron said, "I can't give you the bomb itself. That would be against regulations. However, I can show you how to obtain one yourself." He set his briefcase on the ground, unfastened some straps, reached in and withdrew a sheaf of papers. He ruffled through them until he found the one he wanted. "Here you are," he said.

"Here is what?" Greenberg asked.

"Main line indeed!" I said.

"It's a diagram of a missile silo, located in . . . er . . . that place. And all you have to do is follow this red line here till you reach the bomb and then activate it. It's really quite simple. For a man of your abilities, Tsaddik, there'd be nothing to it. Just think, no more air pollution."

"No more anything," Greenberg said.

I said: "Look. If you're so against that place, why don't you drop the bomb yourself?"

The man called Myron smiled ruefully. "I'd like to," he admitted, "really I would. But it can't be done. I'd never hear the end of it. A violation of Ethical Standards, you know. Positively against regulations. Absolutely. Why, I'd be jailed! No, it's quite out of the question. It must be the work of an indigen. The regulations are quite specific on that."

"Whose regulations?" I inquired.

"The Real Estate Commission. Who else?"

"I see," I said, seeing nothing. We Tsaddikim are not quick to indicate we don't know something.

"And you, sir," Myron said, "are a genuine indigen."

"I *am?*"

"Of course."

"And what am I?" demanded Greenberg.

"You," said Myron, "are obviously an undigested piece of cheese."

"What a humiliation for Greenberg the Homunculus!" Greenberg said.

"No," I said, "I don't think I'm really interested." I shook my head. "It's really not for me, I think."

"Oh, too bad, too bad," Myron said. "I'd had such high hopes."

"I'm not really concerned with the air pollution over there," I said.

"Every citizen should be," Myron pointed out.

"I don't really live there, after all."

"Even visitors."

"And the solution seems so . . . er . . . extreme, you might say."

"Just ignore him, boss," Greenberg said.

"How about some nerve gas?" Myron asked. "Would you prefer that, perhaps? Nerve gas is painless, you know. The other indigens wouldn't feel a thing. I could show you how to get just loads of nerve gas."

"Well . . ." I said. "I *really* don't *think* so; honestly, it's just not the type of thing I'm interested in right now . . . maybe some other time."

"If that's the way you feel about it . . ." Myron said.

"Give him the cold shoulder, bossnik," Greenberg said.

"I'm quite sure," I said.

Myron sighed. "I didn't think it was going to be this easy," he said, "and it isn't." He closed his briefcase, tipped his hat, turned and strolled back behind the mound of bricks.

I waited a minute and then followed him. Naturally there was no one there. "See?" I told Greenberg. "Now tell me we're on the main line."

"We're on the main line."

"So how do you explain that fellow?"

"I'm not in the explaining business; I'm in the traveling business."

Just then a large sun-tanned person clad in a white cotton skirt-like garment and carrying a short, ugly whip came over.

"Hey, guy," he said in the current vernacular. "How come you ain't down there with the other slavies, huh?" He raised his whip.

"Oh-oh," I said, "I'm becoming part of the picture again. Maybe I'd better vanish?"

"Maybe you'd better," Greenberg said.

I did.

The Lund Casebook: One

I came down in a slow, easy glide, as though I were riding the strings of an invisible parachute. It was night; you could hear the crickets chirping away. The place was filled with night noises.

I had materialized only a second before. About six feet above the ground the mechanism seemed to go burp and shorted out. I hit hard, piling up on all fours like a cat. The grass was long, sweet-smelling and covered with dew. I got to my feet slowly, brushing off the moist earth, and looked around. The cool odors of outdoors came to me, drifting in on the breeze.

I had landed in a field somewhere—just a wide field with trees and grass. The standard equipment for this type of world. You've seen one, you've seen them all.

Take it easy, Lund, I said to myself; enjoy it while you can: where you come from there's only the smell of asphalt and heated metal, too much smoke and too much hurry. Live a little, Lund, I said to myself.

Up on the hill was a castle, a man-sized job of brick, stone and mortar, and the high walls around it were meant to discourage would-be climbers. Pointy twin towers rose like mastheads reaching for the stars.

And the screams, I figured, were coming from there.

They were pretty good as screams went. They had the right timbre and breathing control, were coming out well-spaced with just the right touch of urgency and need. It was a woman's voice, and she knew all about screams, had probably done a lot of screaming before.

It was really none of my business, of course.

You've been to a thousand cockeyed worlds and seen and felt and done more things than is good for a man, Lund, I said to myself; you ought to let this ride.

I grinned, remembering the home office dictum:

DON'T MIX WITH THE LOCAL YOKEL.

Sure. It looked swell pinned up on the wall, bordered by a gilt frame, but it wasn't worth a hill of beans when a caseworker hit the field; half the job was getting along with the yokels. Sometimes it made all the difference.

I thumbed open my traveling bag, unhooked the levitator, rose to the castle wall and over it. I pulled short at a convenient open window and saw what I could see.

It was enough.

She had blond hair the color of new-cut hay, and it swirled around her waist as she ran. Her skin was all peaches and cream; her face was flushed: she'd never need make-up and didn't have any on now. I couldn't tell the color of her eyes from where I was but they were probably blue. It added up that way. The dress she wore was pink, long-sleeved, embroidered with white lace and swept across the floor. The skirt was wide, so you couldn't distinguish much of the figure, but I was willing to lay odds it was a knockout.

The guys in there must have thought so too, because they were chasing after her.

They all kept circling this long, bare wooden table that filled the center of the huge, stone-walled hall. There was plenty of room to move about in and the girl was making the most of it. Every once in a while she'd open her pretty lips and try out a series of screams, shrieks and hollers. But it was a losing proposition. There was no future in it.

Sooner or later they'd catch her; that was for sure.

There were six of them working up a sweat, and if they

hadn't been stewed witless they'd have landed her long ago. As it was, they kept tripping over each other and getting in the way of the dangling swords they carried on their belts.

They didn't seem to mind much; it was all, apparently, part of the game. Too bad, but I was going to spoil their fun.

I used the image projector.

The image that sprang through the window was nothing this world had ever seen.

The Mindle is one of the tamer species on Bilck 20; it hardly bothers anyone; it doesn't need to. One look at the Mindle is enough to convince most creatures, no matter how dense, that it's best to head in the opposite direction.

The Mindle began to balloon out as soon as it hit the hall, filling most of it in a matter of seconds. The Mindle is, of course, mostly mouth, and it doesn't take a genius to figure out that with a mouth like that, the Mindle mostly eats. That the Mindle eats only shrubs and grass was no one's business.

The Mindle showed its teeth.

End of act one, scene one.

I stepped through the window and picked the young lady off the floor. She'd done the sensible thing and fainted.

The six heroes had beat it through the nearest doorway.

I looked around for a place to plant sleeping beauty and finally settled on the table. This castle wasn't set up for comfort—that was plain. It must have been hell in winter. I lit a butt while waiting and watched the smoke do tricks.

After a while Cinderella pried open an eyelid. Blue-eyed, what did I tell you?

"Hi, kid," I said.

"*Ungle zemph mump,*" she responded.

"Sorry about that," I said. I switched on the translator.

"Try that again, sweetheart," I told her.

Her lips parted; she spoke:

"Yee ben salt of the erthe that yif the salt shal vanyshe

away, wherynne shal it be saltid? To no thing it is worth over, ni bot that it be sent out, and defouled of men."

"Sure, kid," I said, "just take it easy. No one's going to get hurt. Defouled?" I twisted some more dials on the translator. These translators are finicky gadgets; if you didn't set them just right they could sound pretty awful.

"Try it again, baby," I said.

"Whatcha talkin' about, ya stupie creep ya?"

"Cool it, kid," I said.

I lit a match and held it up to the translator. "We'll get this straightened out yet," I told the girl. I was very careful this time in pointing the dials on the small cube-like device. I squinted at it; there were sure a hell of a lot of dials.

"That should do it," I said finally. "Say something."

The girl sat up on the table. She couldn't have been much older than twenty. Maybe only eighteen.

"Hiya," she said. "You some kind of devil or something?"

That was more like it. I worked a grin. "Only with the ladies, baby," I said.

"Then how come all that smoke?"

Smoke? I was still puffing away at my butt. I showed it to her. "Forget it," I said, "it's only this, see?" I flipped it toward the floor and ground it out with a heel.

Her face lit up. "Hey, that's keen."

"Sure," I beamed. The translator was finally on the job. And about time, too. What the hell, I decided; let's play it straight for once. "I come from another world," I told her simply, wondering how she'd take it.

"Sure you do, honey," she said.

"Who are you, sweetheart?"

"I'm a princess."

Hell, the kid must be in shock. "Take it easy," I told her, rummaging in a pocket, "I've got some pills here that'll fix you up."

"No kiddin'," she said, "I'm a Polish princess."

"Is that so?"

"Honest. And this is my castle." She'd whipped up off the table, stood facing me.

"What's Polish?" I asked her.

"I am."

"What does it mean?" I said.

"It's a country."

"Polish?"

"*Poland.* We know all about the other worlds. Where the gods live and the devils live and the saints live. All that stuff and all the worlds in between too. It's old hat with us Poles," she said.

I got it now. For a while there she'd really had me going.

"Sure, kid," I said, "that's how it is."

She took hold of my arm. "Hey," she said. "Did you make those creeps take a powder?"

"That's right," I told her. "Me and my playmate. He comes from another world, too. Who are those clowns? You being a princess and all, that chasing around doesn't figure."

"Those fellows," she said, "are Teutonic knights. They're *Germans*. Why, there's this terrible war going on all over the land. It's simply awful. I mean, a princess isn't even safe in her own castle anymore." She lowered her voice. "They've all ganged up on poor Casy."

"Casy?"

"Casimir the Fourth, His Royal Highness our King."

I plucked out the *Terra Guide Book* and looked under C: Casimir the Fourth—Co-ords 2.3.46. There he was, all right.

"What do these knights want?" I asked.

"Everything!"

Sure. That figured. It's what's usually wanted.

"What year is this?" I asked.

"Fourteen hundred and fifty-three."

That meant nothing.

I said: "How long's this ruckus been going on?"

She shrugged: "Just forever, it seems like. We kicked their ass once, way back in 1410—"

"Stop," I said. I adjusted the translator, nodded, "Go on."

"It was a *splendid* victory—but we haven't had any lately, and if *you* don't do something quick I'm going to be obscenitied right here in my *own* castle."

"Cut," I yelled, turning the dial. "All right," I said.

"I shall be *violated,* I say—"

I turned the damn dial again.

"Well, that's the straight goods, Jack. You've got to help me."

"Sure," I said.

"Rape, rape, rape," she said.

"I get the picture," I said. "What's your name, kid?"

"Wanda."

"Call me Lund, kid," I said.

"Lund kid," she said.

Just then we heard the racket.

"Sounds like a bunch of tin cans clattering up a flight of stone steps," I observed.

"Very *amusing,*" she said. "You might be interested to know that each can comes equipped with its very own goon. And you know what that means, Lund kid? Rape, rape, rape, hack, hack, hack."

"Let's not get carried away, princess," I told her.

"Hell," she said, "we should of scrammed when we had the chance."

"Let me handle it," I told her.

All at once the fancy plush curtain over the far right archway swung to one side, and half the metal works from the foundry began clanging into the hall.

There were about twenty-six of them, I saw. The clamor we'd heard belonged to their swords, shields and breastplates; they sounded like a plumber's box out for a night on the town. I waved a greeting.

My simple gesture had thrown confusion through the ranks of our visitors, had halted them in their tracks. That and my black-blue uniform, probably. They looked us over, wide-eyed, from a safe distance.

A fat, burly fellow with three dancing chins—a large, hairy wart on one of them—a shiny bald pate and a long, brown coarse robe lumbered forward a few feet. The army chaplain, no doubt.

His chubby fist raised a twelve-inch wooden cross. His hand was shaking but he stood his ground; you had to hand him that. His fat lips quivered: "I, Bulbus the Monk, bid you . . . begone! In the name of . . ." He rattled off a loud string of multisyllabic names. They sounded imposing.

The clump of heroes behind him were huddled together for warmth and comfort, waiting for the names to do their stuff. They didn't look very hopeful.

A big rosy-faced guy in a long green cape—the captain of the guards?—detached himself from the rest of this crew, wearily stepped up behind the monk and, in a surprisingly high-pitched soprano voice, suggested: "We could rush him, chief."

"It would do no good," the monk replied unhappily. "It is well known that spirit beings are immaterial."

"The cross, chief, doesn't seem to function with its . . . er . . . usual efficiency," the big guy pointed out.

Bulbus the Monk thought that one over. "It's probably a Jewish demon," he said in his heavy, rumbling voice. "They've been all over the place recently. Very bad for morale. Perhaps I'd better try a spell or two the rabbi taught me—"

Wanda said: "Wow, if you *are* a devil, Lund kid, you're in big trouble now."

"Quiet," I told her. "I'm trying to memorize all this for my article on indigenous folkways of army chaplains. This is very important."

The monk began to chant:

"Shabriri
briri
riri
iri
ri.

"He should be gone now," the monk sighed. "Especially if his name is Shabriri. Sunk to nothing but a dot."

"He isn't," the captain said.

"I see that, you fool!"

"What should we do?" the captain demanded.

"I must be going," the monk explained. "These Jewish demons are impervious to reason. Besides, it's almost time for vespers."

"It's the middle of the night!"

"Mind your own business," the monk said.

The captain retreated to his men, went into an urgent huddle.

The monk murmured, "Perhaps I should try the old Tetragrammaton incantation. It is obviously not Shabriri . . ."

"How long is this supposed to go on?" Wanda demanded.

"Until he can come up with one that makes me vanish, I suppose."

"How long will that take?"

"Forever, probably."

"That's too long."

The girl was right.

The huddle on the other side of the hall, meanwhile, was almost over. The assorted heroes had begun stealing glances, again, in our direction. They'd made up their minds about something, it appeared.

The captain advanced a few paces. "You there," he called.

"What's on your mind?" I said.

"Are you a devil?" the captain asked. "Are you a spirit, a demon, an imp?"

"That's just for the sucker trade," I said. "Actually I'm pretty regular in my habits."

"We should have brought along some garlic," Bulbus the Monk was saying. "That, or a wolf's tooth. These . . . charms, you know . . . are infallible." He suddenly brightened. "Perhaps I should go fetch some now?"

"We'll try to shoot him first," the captain said. "Archers!"

Four archers stepped forward.

"He might not like it," Bulbus pointed out.

"Well, those are the breaks," the captain said.

"He might do something *bad*," the monk said.

"Could be," the captain acknowledged.

"Bad to *us*," the monk added.

"The hazards of military service," the captain shrugged.

"I'd better go bring some garlic and a wolf's tooth," the monk said.

"The wolf might not like that," I pointed out.

"He's a wise guy," the captain said. "I'm going to shoot him. On the ready!"

The archers readied.

"Oh-oh," Wanda said. "Now look what you've done."

"Wait a minute," I said.

"See? He's begging for mercy already," the captain said. "He's a sissy."

"I can't stand trouble," the monk said. "It's my liver; it's overworked."

"Take aim!" the captain called.

"What if you hit *her?*" the monk asked.

"Too bad," the captain said.

"Hey, you guys, you'd better hold it a minute," I called.

I projected an image:

The dancing girls that appeared between us and the archers took up a lot of floor space. There were about forty of them and they had nothing on. Very exotic.

"Shake it up, girls," I said.

"It's indecent," Wanda said.

"It sure is," I said. All we were getting was a lot of backside.

The girls went into their dance.

The archers lowered their weapons. The monk had both hands over his eyes, but you could tell he was peeking too.

"Two to a customer," I said. "Free of charge, naturally; help yourselves: best buy this side of the Ganges. Step right up, folks; get an eyeful; see for yourselves."

To Wanda I said: "This is probably going to blow your mind, but we're going to fly out the window."

"I can take it," she said. "After this, I can take anything."

I swept an arm around her waist. She nestled against my side, smiled up at me. "You're really something," she said.

"Yeah," I said.

We levitated out the window.

"Namely, the devil," she said.

No one noticed us leave. They were occupied with other matters.

"Let's just skip this devil stuff," I suggested.

The night was spread out below us. We flew over field and valley. The castle was a thing of the past now. There were small hills, and then there was water underneath. We kept on going.

From my traveling bag the directional gizmo was starting to come alive. A low, humming sound emanated from it. Beeps, blops and bloops—we were closing in . . . on something. I made several course changes, found the direction of the signal and headed for it.

Wanda asked, "You got someplace special in mind?"

"Yeah," I said, "we're looking for a leak. A cosmic leak."

"This leak thing bad?"

"Could be. There's something funny about it. It should be more diffuse than this, more spread out. But it isn't. We're headed for one specific spot, and that's not right."

The gizmo started whistling up a tune like a teakettle. We were getting hot.

"What's that?" Wanda asked.

"We're close," I said.

"What happens now?"

"I plug the leak."

"Just like that?"

"Sure. Why not?"

As if in answer, right at that instant, we flew smack into the invisible barrier and went careening—helter-skelter—down.

Courtney: One

Lund was gone.

"What do you mean gone?" I asked Krellech, somewhat irritably. I hate being interrupted. How can a being get anything done with these constant interruptions!

Krellech waved a flapper at me, extended a talk-cube, intoned, "See for yourself, Courtney," placed a voice-slit on my desk and waddled away.

I had been finishing off a report on the Zwigly, trying to explain how the 50,000 tons of Trush we'd sent them, in a radiant outburst of bureaucratic generosity, couldn't possibly grow on a minus 4 world, that if anyone had taken the trouble to glance in the *Outer Galaxies Handbook*, section 12, subheading 9, part b, they'd have known as much, and that if we didn't get rid of the stuff soon, it would probably eat away all the bedrock on the planet, thereby effectively ending the Zwigly problem by ending the Zwigly, when word came about Lund.

I eyed the voice-slit with a mixture of anxiety and distaste. I was behind schedule as it was. This Zwigly thing wasn't even my case. Keinletter had been handling it, when he'd run into some flack on a routine check on Mangus 10. Poor Keinletter. One of the Manguseans had eaten him. Well, these things will happen, of course, even to the best case-worker, but it left me in a hole. Bradley was on vacation; Graves had had himself transferred to Home Economics; Hull had quit; Langley was still recuperating from the trouble he'd had on Yiggle 6 when the natives discovered he wasn't naturally amphibian; Freeman had been promoted to assistant case supervisor in another section. And everyone else was out in the field. There was one desk to the left of me, four to the right and six facing me, and they were *all* empty.

Well, you just had to look around to see it. There wasn't another humanoid in sight. Twelve desks, twelve chairs and just me running the whole show.

The other units down the aisle, manned (or, more properly speaking, bodied) by the furry-toed Nicks, the barrel-shaped Skid, the vine-like Dolophodales and their ilk, couldn't help me a smidgin. They wouldn't know how. It was all specialization these days. And the closest humie unit, four floors away, dealt solely with the Middle Galaxies and had no authority to even *look* at my case records, let alone lend a hand.

Well, there was no putting off the inevitable. Sooner or later it would get me anyway.

I gingerly prodded the voice-slit with a finger, heard it go "grumph," cough and begin to rattle on a mile a minute. Stupid voice-slit!

It was saying: "Honored member of Cosmo Corps, Unit 623, be informed that caseworker Lund has been canceled while in line of field work in Outer Galaxy 59, sector 12, time-space co-ordinates 2.3.49. Immediate replacement urgently required. Report to assistant supervisor at once." The thing went "squinch!" or something like that and added: "You'll no doubt want to avenge your fellow caseworker as soon as possible."

I sat there and glared at it. "Just what do you mean by *avenge?*" I demanded. But it was no use. Avenge meant nothing, and the rest meant I was on the hot seat again. Yes, there you had it. Because "canceled" meant dead and "replacement" meant me. Who else was there?

Only I couldn't go.

It wasn't my turn, by golly. I'd exceed my quota, and the union was dead set against that. Boy, were they strict! If there was one thing a caseworker didn't want to do it was mess around with the old union. And, anyway, my vacation was coming up in only another couple of days.

The voice-slit was beginning to wheeze again. I placed a stack of used case records on it, pushed back my chair, got up and set off for the boss's office. We'd see who they were going to railroad into some backwoods stick-in-the-mud galaxy, by golly.

The Tsaddik Himself: Two

We were on a long line. It was dusk.

We had plenty of time, so we didn't mind waiting.

You could tell by the way the air smelled we were back in that place.

"We're back in that place," I said to Greenberg.

The man ahead of us turned around. "I beg your pardon?" he said.

"Nothing," I said. "I always talk to myself."

The man faced forward again.

"Is he crazy, pop?" a small boy demanded.

"Shut up," the man said, "he'll hear you."

"He must be crazy," the boy concluded. "A lot of people are these days."

"I had it scheduled," Greenberg said.

"It stinks here," I said.

The people up in front stiffened but didn't turn around. The line was moving very slowly.

"This isn't the city," Greenberg said. "You should smell one of their cities."

"Greenberg, I remember."

The woman behind me tapped me on the shoulder. "Mister, who's Greenberg?"

"Should I show her?" Greenberg asked.

"No," I said to Greenberg. To the lady I said, "You can't see him, lady; he's invisible."

The woman sighed. "It's a shame," she said.

"He's not so beautiful," I said.

"You should get help, mister," the woman said.

"But handsome—yes!" Greenberg said.

"In this day and age, people like you can be helped," the woman said.

"Greenberg," I said, "what day and age is this where they can help people?"

"They can't help no one," Greenberg said. "This is Scarsdale. It's June 9, 1986 A.D."

"What's Scarsdale?" I asked.

The woman groaned. "Mister, you're a very bad case."

"Look," I said, "if you can help people, why does it stink so?"

"That's the air pollution," the woman said. "It's got nothing to do with people. It's everywhere."

"Scarsdale is a suburb of New York City," Greenberg said. "It used to house the bigwigs, but now it's a refuge for the hoi polloi."

"Where'd you get *that?*" I asked.

"*American Jewish Yearbook*, 1985."

"What are bigwigs?" I asked.

"Important people in George Washington's time."

"You're crazy!" I said.

"Not me, mister," the woman said. "I've got my mental certificate with me. Where's yours?" She had raised her voice.

The man in front turned around. "Is he bothering you, lady?" he asked.

"He's crazy!" the woman said.

"See?" the boy said "I *told* you. It's a national *affliction*."

"Don't use big words," the man said. "People will think you're different."

"Greenberg, what's a mental certificate?" I asked.

"Overcrowding has made them crazy. Just like with mice."

"Mice?"

"*Where?*" the woman shrieked. "I can't stand mice. Mice make me crazy!"

An old man up in front yelled, "Crazy? Don't use that word crazy. It drives me *crazy*." He swung his cane around wildly.

"When you put a lot of mice together in a narrow space, it drives them crazy," Greenberg explained. "It was a famous experiment. Mental certificates are to show how much people are crazy: a lot or a little."

The people on line were beginning to murmur and mumble. The line was still moving very slowly. Some people left the line to peer up ahead and see what the delay was. Others had begun to push a little bit. The line swayed.

"Push back if they get nasty," Greenberg said. "It's the only language they understand."

"Do I have a mental certificate?" I asked Greenberg.

"I don't remember. Look in your pocket."

"You're in big trouble if you don't know," the man in front told me.

I put my hand in my pocket and pulled out a frog. I looked at it. The frog looked at me. "Uh-uh," I said. "I don't like this."

"What have you got there?" the man in front asked. "What the *hell* have you got there?"

"Something's wrong," Greenberg said. "*That* doesn't belong here."

"It's a frog," I said.

"It's a *meeskite*," Greenberg said.

We had been waiting in line at a temple to get tickets for one of their services. It wasn't as big as the temple in Egypt. This temple was different. It was a small neighborhood temple.

A man stuck his head out of the temple door, grinned, hung a sign on a nail.

The sign read:

CLOSED FOR THE HIGH HOLIDAYS.

"What do I do with the frog?" I asked Greenberg.

"Put it back in your pocket," Greenberg said. "This is all wrong."

"I'll let it go," I said. "What high holidays?"

Greenberg shrugged. "There aren't any. It's a mistake."

I put the frog down on the ground. "Beat it, frog," I said. The frog just sat there and looked at me.

"We're in trouble," Greenberg said.

The line was breaking up. People were slowly wandering off in all directions.

"What should we do?" I asked.

"We're in the middle of a mistake," Greenberg said. "You should pardon me."

Myron the Salesman stepped out from behind a tree. "My goodness," he said, "I had a simply awful time running you down. What are you doing way out *here*?"

"Consider yourself pardoned," I said to Greenberg. To Myron I said, "Hello. So you're back again?"

"I had an inspiration," Myron said.

"So let's hear it," I said.

"Poison," Myron said.

"That's your inspiration?" Greenberg said.

"What about it?" I asked.

"You could put it into the drinking supply."

"I don't think so," I said, shaking my head. "Thanks anyway, but I'm really not interested right now."

"Are you positive?"

"Maybe some other time," I said.

"It's getting dark," Greenberg said.

"And just how do you plan to get out of *here*?" Myron asked.

"It's getting very dark," I agreed.

"We gave already," Greenberg said. "Go away."

"You'll see," Myron said.

"I think the world is winking out," I said.

"Don't get excited," Greenberg said.

Myron went away somewhere. I didn't see where. Everything else went away too.

It was extremely dark.

I seemed to be standing on a little round ball somewhere. Emptiness was everywhere else.

"That's the world you're standing on," Myron's voice said.

"Greenberg!" I said.

"Maybe you should work a little wonder," Greenberg said.

"What kind?" I yelled. "Look, you're the travel *mavin;* you get me out of here."

"We're not on the main line," Greenberg said worriedly. "Don't do nothing, like take a step. You could fall off. It's sure dark down there. Just hold on now. I'm doing something—"

Rabbi Issac ben Rubin trotted for home. The cobblestones seemed to dance under his feet, and the little two-story dingy frame houses that lined both sides of the shtetl street seemed to shake with wordless merriment. Ben Rubin knew the laughter was all in his mind, and that made it all the worse: one minute in your mind; the next, out on the street chasing after you. That was the trouble, all right: people had forgotten how to control their minds; they'd lost the knack. It was the scourge of the age.

A knight galloped by on a large white klink, his armor gleaming brightly in the noonday sun. Exhaust fumes poured out of the klink's rear end fume tube, leaving a black, oily stink behind it. The rabbi coughed and shook a fist at the swiftly departing figure.

"*Shlemiel,*" he muttered. This klink fad would go too far one of these days and smell up the whole world.

Even a man of the rabbi's prodigious talents wasn't safe

out on the streets anymore. But then, a person couldn't stay locked up at home all day, anyway, even if it would do any good—which it wouldn't. Besides, the rabbi felt certain he could handle anything that might come his way. *Anything*.

As soon as he had this thought he knew it for the error it was. *Chutspahdik*. It could only lead to bad trouble.

It did.

When the Wenzel appeared on the far side of the street, the rabbi was prepared. The Wenzel was big as a tree, but uglier.

Green flames shot from its flaring nostrils. Its scaly hide was a cluster of unsightly blemishes. It reared up on its ponderous hind legs and blundered toward the rabbi, emitting an unnerving assortment of grunts, groans, wheezes and squeals. Fortunately, as Wenzels went, it was a rather commonplace Wenzel, a third-rate Wenzel, in fact, and the rabbi dispatched it with a well-aimed lightning bolt between its bloodshot eyes. The lightning bolt was first-rate, in fact. The Wenzel went puff. There was only black, oily smoke.

Father O'Malley appeared at the rabbi's elbow. "Just between you and me, rabbi," he whispered, "we seem to have a bit of a pollution problem on our hands. Wouldn't you say?"

The rabbi fanned away the smoke with an open palm. "*Hubris*," he explained sadly.

"Ah!" Father O'Malley shook his head and vanished.

The ground opened up under the rabbi's feet just then, and he fell down a gaping hole. His white beard whistled through the air and his long garment fluttered around his knees. A glowing, luminous sign, pointing down, read:

THIS WAY TO THE END.

That wasn't where the rabbi wanted to go.

He created a locomotive and rode up the side of the wall.

Why a locomotive? he wondered.

Black, oily smoke poured from the engine. Ah! the rabbi

thought bitterly. He began to see the pattern. It all had to do with the klink. The key design centered around . . . *exhaust.* It was always good to know the key design, even if it didn't help any. And it almost never did. The rabbi sighed. He wondered how much of this was the product of his own mind and how much the result of external, natural forces.

The rabbi abandoned the locomotive, which promptly disintegrated; he sprouted wings and flew the rest of the way to the surface. The wings gave off a black, oily smoke. An *unshikenish,* the rabbi thought grimly. The protective spell he'd worked up against (and what else could it be but) *instant retribution* was doing its best, but it was discouraging to see how a little retribution always managed to leak through.

The scene that greeted the rabbi on the surface was quite different from the one he had expected to find.

Towering mounds of candy were everywhere. The town, all four blocks of it, was gone.

The rabbi was astounded. Tampering with permanent places wasn't allowed. For one wild moment he considered the possibility that this was some continuation of his own *tsures.* But that couldn't be. The key design, the pattern was wrong. . . .

This was something else, and the rabbi thought he knew *what.*

The wings on his shoulder blades dropped away as he cast an anxious eye around him. It didn't take long to trace the mischief to its source. Long years of experience had perfected the rabbi's divining powers; besides, there were footprints that could be followed.

The two brown-eyed, curly-haired mites he found skulking behind a hill of disgustingly sweet candies tried to ward him off with spells of their own—naturally—but the youngsters were no match for the old necromancer. There was only one thing to do and the rabbi did it. He became the Spanker! a huge brute in a ragged leopard skin and with very large hands

. . . after a while the two culprits—offspring of a neighboring shtetl—were persuaded to return the town to its proper shape and were sent on their way. The rabbi, ultimately, could have done it himself, of course, but, since he lacked the key to the spell, it might have taken weeks, or even months. Frankly, he didn't feel up to it.

Wearily, the rabbi continued on his way home. Working spells took something out of a man. It almost paid, sometimes, to have the work done by a commercial outfit, only you never knew where you stood with those fellows. First, their prices were always exorbitant, and, second, you could never count on the quality. The rabbi labored up a short hill, wheezing to himself. There was no escape, he thought, with things the way they were these days. It was better to do it yourself. Be sure of the product.

Those kids should have known better than to change the shtetl. True, it was only a showpiece . . . so people wouldn't forget what a shtetl looked like—no one lived there—but the regulations against tampering were strict. A national monument: The Typical Modern Shtetl, it was meant as a guide for people who might want to create their own shtetl someday. . . You could never tell, unlikely as it seemed; somebody might want to do it. . . . After all, people were funny. Yes, the *permanent places* had to be preserved; the rules said so, otherwise there'd be chaos.

"Yoo hoo," a voice yelled.

"Huh?"

"Over here."

"Where?"

"In the hole."

"Hole?"

"Look down. By your right foot."

"Over here?"

"Yeah. You see me now?"

"Wait, I'll get down on my hands and knees."

"Oy, what a trip I've had."
"There you are. What are you, some kind of earth spirit?"
"It's me. Greenberg."
"Greenberg?"
"Hold tight, nitwit."

We were sitting on a rock in a green pasture. There were hills and clouds.
"Hello, Greenberg," I said.
"I think I've got heartburn," Greenberg said. "Could you make, maybe, an Alka-Seltzer?"
I went *puff*.
"Thank you," Greenberg said. He downed the drink, smacked his lips, stretched. "So what's new?" he said.
I sighed.
"I get the general idea," Greenberg said.
"I went *third person*," I said.
"No kidding?" Greenberg said.
"Greenberg, I didn't even know I was *me*."
"It happens now and then. So what?"
"What was it, Greenberg?"
"Ah ha!" Greenberg said.
"You know?" I asked, with hope.
Greenberg shrugged. "Who knows anything?"
"I had a long, white beard," I said, "and I was a rabbi."
"Mazel tov."
I fingered my chin. No beard. Issac to normal. In our shtetl, everyone is a tsaddik, but no one wears a beard. There aren't any rabbis. It's a very peculiar shtetl.
"Where are we?" I asked Greenberg.
"You don't recognize the place?"
I looked around. "It looks familiar," I admitted.
"We're outside Muddle."
Muddle was our very own shtetl. "Can you imagine that?" I said, with some wonder.

"Why not?" Greenberg said. "I did it, didn't I?"

"Can you beat that," I said, trying out some twentieth-century vernacular.

"I could, maybe, sing a song for an encore."

"We'd better get back to Muddle," I said finally.

"What's the rush?"

"Why not?"

I started walking across the field, Greenberg on my right shoulder.

It was a clear day, beautiful early spring. The grass had just come out. The trees were beginning to blossom. The sky was blue and cloudless. The ground was flat and level here; farther on you could see the small green hills rising. An occasional bird fluttered by. A mild breeze brought the odor of flowers with it. I was beginning to feel uneasy.

"We'll have to be more careful in future trips. We don't want an epidemic of *third person.*"

"I'll look into it," Greenberg said.

"Third person is terrible," I said. "It's a beautiful day."

"It sure is."

"I've never seen it quite this beautiful."

"Not this close to Muddle," Greenberg agreed.

"Really magnificent," I said.

"Extraordinary," Greenberg said.

We came to a winding, narrow dirt road. I started hiking down the road. I hurried.

"*Ah mekhiya,*" Greenberg said, "to get away from all that air pollution, ha?"

"It's funny," I said.

"Hysterical," Greenberg said. "What is?"

"There was air pollution back in that third-person place."

"It's everywhere," Greenberg agreed.

"It was part of the pattern," I said.

"What pattern?" Greenberg said.

I said, "I'm not sure. There was a model shtetl, too."

"What for?"

"In case anyone wants to create his own shtetl. Although it seems unlikely. To say the least."

"It must have been like home."

"There were no tall buildings," I said.

"Who needs 'em? *Narishkiyten* . . ."

"And not one woman!"

"What? Are they crazy? What kind of a terrible place was this? No women? Whoever heard of such a thing? It's a disgrace! A place like that will never get anywhere. No wonder no one goes there."

"There was a monster."

"Now *that* sounds like Muddle."

"That's my point."

"I see what you mean," Greenberg said uneasily. "No monsters in sight."

"Precisely. Whoever heard of it being peaceful this close to Muddle."

"No one!" Greenberg shouted.

"Look at the sky. Look at the grass. Look at the trees!"

"It's idyllic!" Greenberg groaned.

"*Oy vey!*" I cried. "Something *terrible* must have happened!"

I started to run along the winding path. I rounded a bend, and the shtetl walls were visible in the distance.

"Make a wonder," Greenberg shouted.

"We're almost there," I yelled.

"Hurry, hurry," Greenberg urged.

"I'm hurrying," I pointed out.

I peered ahead at our little shtetl, Muddle, and it seemed serene and peaceful, nestled in the lap of green rolling vegetation. Green vines grew up the sides of the walls.

"Watch it! Those may be snakes," Greenberg warned.

Not a leaf or blade of grass seemed out of place and whoever heard of that, this close to Muddle?

"Do you hear any screams for help?" I yelled. "Gun shots? Bombs?"

"Don't be silly," Greenberg said. "That would be normal."

He was right. "This must be a terrible, terrible crisis," I yelled.

"The worst!"

"Disastrous."

"The end."

"What should we do?"

"Don't worry," Greenberg said, "I'll think of something."

We were almost at the gate now. It was closed, I saw. We'd have to fly over, unless someone opened it.

"What time is it?" I asked Greenberg. "What day is it?"

"The same day we left—only later."

"On the main line?"

"This is it. Our shtetl. Muddle. The one we left only this morning. I guarantee it. I've been in the travel business a long time. I know my way around. This is Main Line, May 9, 1452 A.D. And we're back home."

Home, I thought. Who needs it?

Courtney: Two

Assistant Case Supervisor Shmelk looked tired. His hair had all but fallen out, and what was left was a mousy gray. His face was lined; his stomach bulged; his chest was sunken; he wore large thick glasses and was almost blind, and he had a terrible cough. Otherwise, he was fine. As a matter of fact, he was doing pretty well for an assistant supervisor. For an assistant supervisor, he was a model of health and stamina. For anyone else, though, he'd have been dead. Whenever I went to his office, I was always careful not to bump him or make loud vibrations with my lips. I had enough on my conscience without knocking off poor old Shmelk. He was all that stood in the way of us caseworkers and Floor Supervisor Velk the Gazoom, and, while it has never been proven that the Gazoom eat their firstborn, neither has it been proven that they *don't*.

"Courtney, lad, is that you? Stop hiding."

"I'm over here, Mr. Shmelk, in the light."

"What's that? Oh! I thought you were lurking in the shadows, lad. Sit down."

"I am sitting down."

"So you are."

"Over here, Mr. Shmelk. That's the bookcase."

"Bookcase?"

"Why don't you put on your glasses, Mr. Shmelk?"

"Put on my—why, yes, that's a thought. Now, where are they? Inkwell, paper clips, Jiffy Pen and Pencil Set, yo-yo, ah! Here they are. Glasses! Puts a new light on things. Now,

Courtney, let's get down to brass tacks: why have you sent for me?"

"It's the other way around, Mr. Shmelk."

"It is? How peculiar. Perhaps I was feeling lonesome. It gets lonely here. It's my stomach, you know, a cause of constant concern. Many think, no doubt, that an assistant case supervisor's lot is all roses and soda-water—"

"Lund, sir."

"What's that, lad? What was that naughty word?"

"Lund!"

"Good gracious, that *is* what you're here for, isn't it?"

"I'm afraid so."

"This terrible Lund business! I might as well tell you that Gazoom Velk saw me this morning, and he was *very* upset."

"Probably wanted to eat you. You're not a firstborn, I take it?"

"For gracious sake, keep your voice down, lad; he's only down the hall; don't you know the Gazoom hearing—"

The door popped open. A large shaggy fur-covered head stuck itself into the room, looked around quickly, opened its mouth, let out a wall-shaking growl and withdrew.

"Now look what you've gone and done," Shmelk said.

"Gazoom Velk's in good voice today."

"He can always tell when his name is being mentioned. Telepathic on that one point, you know. Dear me, dear me. He seemed a bit perturbed, wouldn't you say?"

"Yeah. I'd say that. Sure. Why not?"

"It's this Lund business. It's got us all in a tizzy."

"Not me, it ain't, boss. That's what I've come here to tell you. It's not that I don't feel the deep loss of caseworker Lund. Boy, do I feel it. I'm carrying the whole unit by myself! But get this, boss—ninety-two field trips per cycle, according to section 9, clause 20, of the good old union contract is all we get to make. And I've already reached that good old number. That's why, in fact, I've got all this vacation time coming."

"You could always waive section 9, clause 20. . . ."

"Sure. Sure I could. I could also put in for a mind re-vamp at the local clinic while I'm at it. But I won't."

"There's bylaw 74, you know."

"Well, everyone knows that. You think I'd forget that, Mr. Shmelk? Bylaw 74 is engraved in all our hearts, but you'd have to prove, somehow, that old 74 is applicable to the situation."

"It is when there's a 695B!"

"A 695B!"

"Now you *know*, Courtney."

"Like hell, I know. Just what is a 695B?"

"World cancellation, of course."

"*What did you say?*"

"A 695B is a world cancellation."

"That's what I thought you said."

"So you see—"

"Now, come on, Shmelk; let's cut out this horsing around. I wasn't born yesterday, you know. There hasn't been a world cancellation in thousands of cycles. Everyone knows that. Why, even the Cosmos Corps isn't stupid enough to set one of those things in motion. It takes a cosmic leak to just start the thing going. And then you'd need a rupture in the space-time continuum to keep it up. Right?"

"I'm afraid so."

"And you mean to tell me—"

"Lund's mission in Outer Galaxy 59, sector 12, time-space co-ords 2.3.49, was to check on a suspected leak. Cosmo graphs had indicated the possibility of leak activity at that juncture. Lund's last contact with us was a hyper-tape. You've heard it, I believe. That's the last we heard from him, poor chap. Naturally, his interjection into that galaxy, sector and t-s slot in the presence of a cosmic leak constituted a rupture of the space-time continuum. By itself, this would hardly matter. Any qualified caseworker could easily rectify that condition by simply finding and plugging the leak. Unfortunately, Lund's untimely demise puts us in a rather awkward position. There is no one, repeat, absolutely no one on the scene at this moment seeing to the necessary details. The world of galaxy 59, sector 12, time-space co-ords 2.3.49, is headed straight for cancellation. In about forty-eight hours. A 695B automatically results in a bylaw 74. You know that, of course?"

"How the hell should I know *that*? I didn't even know what a 695B was. There hasn't been one in eons."

"Well—you know now, Courtney. Automatic, you see. No question about old 74. It sticks."

"I'll fight it!"

"Of course you will. But I wouldn't if I were you. It would be a mistake."

"Mistake? Mistake? You can't buffalo me, Shmelk. I know my rights."

"No one doubts that, Courtney, but listen—it would be to your a*dvantage* not to make us press this thing. Not to have us invoke 74. Naturally it'd be open and shut in view of the facts. We'd get our way in the end. But it would take time. It would just cut down on your operational span. And you'd gain nothing by it. But if you'd voluntarily waive section 9, clause 20, thereby undertaking to exceed your quota of ninety-two field trips by one—if, I say, you did that and successfully completed your mission—"

"You mean, didn't get canceled out."

"Er . . . yes, and plugged the leak, you'd be in line for—"

"A rest cure."

"A five-rating jump."

"I would?"

"You'd make quite a pretty bundle on that deal. If you volunteered—"

"And if I got back to collect."

"Now, now, what kind of talk is that for a potential hero of the corps?"

"Me? Hero of the corps?"

"A 695B, Courtney, remember that. And, of course, if you don't waive your rights . . . er . . . volunteer, why, we make you go anyhow. Ah, without recompense, naturally. You see?"

"That's quite a choice there, Mr. Shmelk; yessir."

"Don't lose your big opportunity, Courtney lad. This could mean the top for you!"

"Yeah! What's so great about putting my neck in a sling for a lousy five ratings? What does that come down to in prickels and glit? Why a hundred and thirty prickels more a Zwif, that's all . . . say, that *is* a lot, isn't it?"

"A fortune, comparatively speaking. But that's the way of the galaxy, ah, lad?"

"Look—tell me, who takes over the unit if I go? Who worries about the poor old Zwigly if I go, huh? Someone's got to take over the unit."

"We'll have a flox do it."

"A flox? Ech!"

"Now, now, they're trained, you know, to take over in a pinch."

"A flox! Is that the best you can do? We caseworkers aren't much, I'll grant you, but we do have *some* empathy with our *clients*, after all. A flox!"

"Even flox have to pass the civil humility exam, Courtney. They're humble."

"Yeah, but they're not *human!*"

"Who is, these days?"

"They have no feelings."

"They don't need any. It's only a job."

"Our unit handles humie worlds. How can you sic a flox on 'em?"

"I can do anything—unless there's some rule against it. There's no rule against flox."

"Flox smell and look like seaweed!"

"Quiet, lad. There's some genuine seaweed around these halls and they hate being compared to flox."

"Look, Shmelk, have a heart. You're a humie; why don't you take over the unit? It's only for a couple of days."

"*Me?* Take over the unit? My *dear* chap! I'm an *Assistant Case Supervisor!* Who would take over *my* duties?"

"Just what *are* your duties, Shmelk?"

"Let's not get personal, caseworker Courtney. Just run along down to the field office and get yourself outfitted. You're not a hero of the corps yet, fellow."

"Somehow I don't think I'm going to *like* this trip."

"Now, now, Courtney. Chin up. And good luck, lad. You'll probably need it."

A buzzer sounded. Shmelk reached for the viewer. "What?" he said. "Remarkable!" To me he said, "Guess what? Another report has just turned up from poor old canceled Lund; delayed in passage, it seems. Well, these will, no doubt, *really* be his last words. You'll want to hear them, I'm sure."

The Lund Casebook: Two

"Crash landing," I said; "hold tight."

Below us was the night.

And the fires.

Hundreds of campfires licked at the darkness, burned holes in the night.

Before us was the barrier.

The girl had her arms wound tight around my shoulders; her body, full, warm and pulsing, was pressed against mine. Her lips were bent toward my ear; her voice was low and husky as she whispered: "*Heelpp!!!*"

"Quiet," I said.

"I've changed my mind," she said. "I'd rather go back to the castle. It was a hard decision to reach, of course, but I think I'll let those Germans hack me to pieces, after all. It's probably very dull being a German."

The wind, meanwhile, wailed around us like a motherless infant in need of a quick diaper change.

The directional gizmo was carrying on like a fat man with heartburn: a hundred and one grunts, grumps and tinkles were issuing from its speak-tube.

We're here, I thought.

On the spot.

Somewhere nearby I'd find the leak. As soon as I figured out what this barrier was all about.

Don't sweat it, Lund, I said to myself. You can lick it. No matter what it comes down to, you've got the know-how, the training; in a pinch there's always the training, the drill. The long, back-breaking hours put in at cracking a thousand cases. What does it add up to, Lund, I asked myself. A hundred vacations with pay, that's what. But would it be enough to see me through now?

My feet touched ground.

Wanda unwound herself from me.

"Now what?" she said.

"Who belongs to those campfires?"

"Search me."

"Not now. Okay, we'll ignore them."

"That's talking," she said; "let's beat it, huh? I know this great place—we can really have a ball; no one ever goes there."

"Where is it?"

"It's a cave. I can show you."

"A cave? What's so special about that?"

"Well, with all these wars we've been having, we're plum out of resort areas. It's private."

"Yeah. Now let's keep it quiet for a while; we don't want to tip our mitt to the natives. Just help me feel around the air here till we hit the barrier."

"You don't miss a trick, do you?"

"That's what I get paid for, sweetheart," I told her.

We started hunting the barrier.

Something went bump in the dark.

"Is that you, sweetheart?" I said.

"You bet, honey," a gruff male voice replied.

I ducked. Something swung past my head.

I kicked out with a foot, met air, fell down.

It was just as well.

Something dived at where I was an instant ago.

I rolled over.

Footsteps came running toward us from far away.

I crawled out of the way. Let them go chase themselves. I

wasn't getting paid enough to take a beating. I was only a caseworker—not some kind of gladiator nut.

That's when Wanda started to scream. I gave a listen. Not bad. The girl had talent. Only her performance was queering my racket.

I got to my feet and trotted over to the sound effects.

A knot of dark shadows was wrestling around.

I grabbed one by the neck. I swung a fist. The shadow crashed to the ground.

"Pipe down," I told Wanda.

"Eeek!" she said.

"Not so loud," I said. "Eeck quicter." I chopped away at another assailant. He ran off into the night.

"I'll try," she said, "but it won't be easy."

A third figure didn't wait to be hit—prudent fellow—and made tracks on his own.

For the time being we were alone, it seemed.

"Hang loose, kid," I said.

"Ech!"

"I'll admit," I said, "it was touch and go there for a while, but we ran them off."

"Gurgle."

"Gurgle? What kind of talk is that?"

"I've got her by the throat, friend," a rough voice said. "Maybe I'll kill her and maybe I won't; it depends on my mood, friend . . . and on how you behave." A rugged male voice chuckled in the dark.

"Oh, I wouldn't do that, pal," I said.

"You wouldn't, friend?"

"Never."

"Why not, friend?"

That needed some answering.

"You a Pole or a German?" I asked.

"Waddya think, friend; a Pole, what else?"

That made it easier. I had the answer.

"That's Princess Wanda you've got there, bird brain," I said.

"That's a howl," the gruff voice chortled. "Princess Wanda."

"Laugh it up, pal, but wait till the king hears about this."

"Princess Wanda, huh?"

"Can't you tell by the way she's gurgling?" I demanded. "That's royal blood."

"She ain't bleedin'—yet."

I struck a match. "See for yourself, pal," I said.

He was a big lug, all right.

"Go on, friend," he said. "I wouldn't know this Princess Wanda from a hole in the ground. Waddya think I am, some kind of knight or somethin'? I'm just a peasant—that's all, and as humble as they come. There ain't none humbler, you can take it from me—"

The match went out.

I levitated up behind him.

"The school of hard knocks was all the learnin' I got," he was saying.

"Right," I said. I conked him from behind.

"How about that?" he said. "There's two of 'em." He fell down.

Wanda said: "Gasp."

"Sure, kid, you'll be okay now."

Wanda said, "Rasp, cough, cough."

"Easy does it," I said.

"You sure take your bloody time saving a body."

"It was dark. You didn't want to get slugged by mistake, did you?"

"Slugged or strangled—I'll think it over."

"It won't happen again," I assured her.

"You're damn right, because I'm going home; this game is for the birds."

"Just stick with me, kid," I said. "You'll get to like it."

"You're a mad, impetuous dreamer. Say—look over there."

I turned and saw them. There were a few hundred of them with torches and swords, and they were headed this way.

"It's time to go for a spin, huh?" Wanda said.

"Uh-uh."

"Uh-uh?"

"We'll wait and see what they want," I said.

"He's got rocks in the head."

"Well, we'd just have to come back anyway, sweetheart. The barrier's right here somewhere. And that's the point of interest now. Once we polish off this job—"

"What's this 'we' stuff? You starting an agency or something?"

"I'll ignore that—anyway, I plug the leak and we can have some good times, baby."

"This I've got to see."

"Maybe the natives can be some help," I said, "but we'll need a convincer."

"Hey, that skinny guy in the middle there—that's King Casy. Hey, now!"

"The one with the long sword? He doesn't look well fed."

I worked the image projector.

The army that rose up out of the darkness behind me was hardly one from the fifteenth century or these co-ords or even this world. But it was the only army I had handy in the image projector. It would do. It's not so much the getup or hardware that makes for an impression as the look of steely determination on the faces of the combatants. These boys really looked determined. This image was taken just before the whole gang was wiped out on a world called Klint some five centuries ago.

King Casimir the Fourth halted a safe distance from us, raised a hand in greeting.

"Hail," he said.

"Snow, rain and flowers," I said, using the standard reply of Splink 5.

"Jeez," Wanda said, "don't you know *anything?*" To the king she said, "Oh hail, Your Greatness and Mightiness."

The king twitched a narrow shoulder, swallowed; his adam's apple bobbed up and down.

"So," he said, "the enchantment speaks."

Wanda said: "No, it's really me."

"And the devil," he said.

"Let's not start that again," I protested. To Wanda I said, "Okay, let's see you explain me."

"Forget it, Lund kid. I've just retired. I only do the impossible, not the inconceivable."

"Quitter," I sneered. To Casy I said: "Don't let this getup bug you, sire, baby; underneath it all I'm just plain folks."

"And those?" he said, indicating my mass warrior image. "The ungodly host!"

"Now don't get steamed up, sire," I said, "I can explain everything. Watch."

I switched off the image.

The king swayed. "Saints preserve us," he said.

What had been a faintly lit spread of restless men, grim-faced, grime-smeared and menacing, rising silently out of the waist-high grass, was now—nothing.

"You've heard of magicians, sire," I cheerfully told the king, "well, that's me. There are good and bad magicians, of course; everyone knows that. You can put me down as one of the good ones. Just ask the young lady here."

"He's very good," she said.

"Those men," I continued, "were just some of the boys. I always bring them along with me in case there's some kind of trouble. But then trouble, sire, is something—"

"Something unnecessary?" the king asked, hopefully.

"Well put, sire. I was just about to make that very point. Right, sweetheart?"

"He's *very* good," sweetheart said. "Although, truthfully, most of it's just hearsay, so far."

"We'll have some great times together, Wanda, baby," I assured her. To the king I said, "Now, what's all this fuss about? Wanda tells me you've been having some kind of difficulties."

The king tried a smile. It looked more like the grin on an iodine bottle.

"Nothing much," he said, "nothing we can't really handle. What's happened to your men?"

"I've sent them to the in-between world. We magicians can do that, you know. They just wait around there till I need them—the whole bunch. Armed to the teeth, of course. They kill at the drop of a hat. Bloodthirsty crew. Uncontrollable in the heat of battle. Frankly, I'd just as soon keep them in the in-between world. There's no telling what they might do if they get riled up."

"You should keep them there," the king nodded. "Yes, indeed, we fully agree. Our royal heart goes out to you, sir, for your kind, generous . . . er . . . unprecedented offer of assistance—but, in truth, we'd . . . er . . . rather do it ourselves. Why don't you just run along. The last time something like this happened, we had the black death on our hands for years."

I projected an image.

"The ungodly host!" the king shrieked. His men shrank back.

The tall grasses rocked in the wind, and thousands of silent, tight-lipped, deadly men rocked with it, their eyes fixed hungrily on the king.

The image projector came with a voice. I activated it:

A roar went up from my phantom crew. They hefted their weapons: sound rays, light beams and disintegrators. I didn't know what his royal highness would make of those; he was still in the boy scout stage of armaments, but I figured the noise would be enough to throw a scare into him. It was.

His legs buckled; his own men turned tail and vanished into the night. The king was left alone; he made the sign of the cross, said:

"We've kept a list of all our grievous deeds. We'll make amends. No kidding. We can go on long fasts and give a lot to charity and not incite the royal hounds on the serfs anymore; we can mortify our flesh by sticking pins in it and rolling in the snow naked in winter. Oh gracious, there's so much a king can do if he just puts his mind to it. We've been bad, but we're going to be good from now on. We'll cut out sex on Sunday and go to church instead. We will. We'll set an example. We won't have any seconds of dessert at the round table. Now we'll close our eyes and all this will go away. Send the black plague or something, Lord; something we can understand. But not this. Make this go away. Thank you, Lord; just a friendly prayer from your servant, King Casimir the Fourth."

"Don't bother," I told him.

"He's all worked up," Wanda said. "Poor dear."

All this time the king had remained at shouting distance. Now Wanda and I went over to him.

"See," he said, "we've got our eyes closed. They've gone away. We know they've gone away. We sires are good at judging when things go away. All we've got to do is keep our eyes closed. They'll stay away."

"Sire," I said.

"O sire," Wanda said.

"Vile enchantments," the king said, bitterly. "Will you thus mock a king's deepest beliefs?"

I corrected the translator:

"Ya creeps ya . . ." he said.

This translator would have to go.

"Look, King Casy," I said, "we'll be gone soon enough. All we want are some facts."

"That's all," Wanda said, "just the facts."

The king opened his eyes. "That's all you want? Nothing more? Like our royal soul or a pound of flesh or something."

"Hardly," I said with dignity.

"We can go along with that," the king said. "Facts are cheap."

This is more like it, Lund, I said to myself. There's nothing like a little muscle to make the natives go help-happy. This lad is just top dog of a two-bit burg. Let's not waste more time putting on a sideshow; let's get the goods and blow.

"What's the scare here, kingy," I asked. "What gives?"

"You can tell him, sire," Wanda said. "He's good magic."

"You'd better believe it," I said.

"We do!" the king said. "Oh, indeed we do."

"Swell," I said. "Now let's hear you talk it up for the good guys. Spill it, kingy."

"It's the enchantment right over there," the king said, pointing. "About four yards to the right. You can't miss it. Actually, sir, it seems no one can miss it. Knights and peasants just go riding into it. You can't get past it, sir; it's an authentic enchantment. We had Bulbus the Monk authenticate it just yesterday."

"That's the barrier," I told the king.

"We've noticed," he said. "And it's simply got to go. Think what it'll do to commerce, to picnics, athletic events, not to mention our reputation as a clean, decent place to bring up children."

I asked: "How long's this been this way?"

He shrugged. "It came to our royal attention but recently."

"Like when?"

"Last week."

That told me nothing. This barrier could have been here

years, months or weeks. It could have gone unnoticed—and that would have been no great trick. This track of woods was in the middle of nowhere. Folks didn't come here. But it was tied, in some way, to the leak—that much was clear—but just how or why was another matter. One thing was sure: According to corps data, this leak had been around some; it was no new occurrence. And there was danger in that. These leaks had a way of getting out of hand.

"It's not yours?" the king asked.

"This barrier?"

"You're not responsible?"

"What would I want with a barrier?"

"What would anyone?"

The monarch had a point.

I told him: "Barriers aren't my racket, sire; to tell the truth, I've come here to fix this thing."

"It's out of order?"

"To get rid of it, kingy," I explained.

"That would be nice," the king said.

"Just what are you going to do?" Wanda wanted to know.

"I don't know yet," I said.

"There've been sightings," the king said. "Devils and witches and goblins."

"You can forget about that," I said. "Devils aren't real."

"They aren't? Dear us."

"They're mythological beings."

"What about the others?"

"What others?"

"The strange ones in peculiar garb, in outlandish costumes?"

"You've seen 'em?"

"We're looking at 'em."

"Besides me."

"There've been stories . . ."

"What's in a story?"

"It just adds to our kingly problems, which, you know, sir, are nothing to sneer at. We have responsibilities. Cardinal Olesnicki blames these apparitions on the Jews. He wants us to take away their privileges."

"So?"

"The country will go to the dogs if we did that. And the gentry wants us to forbid Jews to own land—or they won't assist us in our wars. Olesnicki says we're impairing the interests of the church. He wants Jews to wear special garments that will distinguish them from Christians. People will be able to run away when they see one coming. Demands, demands . . ."

"What are these privileges you're supposed to take away?"

"Oh, just the usual ones: free trade, religious freedom, things like that . . . things everyone else in these parts has. We Poles are pretty liberal in this day and age. It's made us rich."

"Sure. But can you keep it up?" I asked.

"Olesnicki says the Jews plot from *behind* the barrier. If he has his way we go back to the customs of the good old days."

"How were they?"

"*Terrible!*"

"I'll do what I can, of course."

"Everyone was poor—impoverished."

"We caseworkers always do what we can."

"You've got to be crazy to want to go back to the good old days."

"Caseworkers are like doctors in many ways—only we tend worlds instead of persons."

"Phooey on the good old days!" The king shook a fist.

"Caseworkers guard the galaxies."

"You talk pretty good for an enchantment," the king said.

"Enough chit-chat," I said. "We get to work now."

"Do you know," the king said, "in these parts kings are elected. It's true. We could have run for some other office—"

While the king was mulling over his lost opportunities, I went up to the barrier and laid a hand on it. I pushed it—unyielding. As expected. It was invisible. The roads and fields, the trees and streams, all continued behind it. But the whole territory was locked up, unreachable.

I got the directional finder out and gave it a twist. It merely verified what I already knew: to get to the leak, I'd have to cross the barrier.

The king and Wanda watched me as I worked.

The king said: "It's back to the dark ages if we don't scratch this barrier angle."

I fixed the translator.

"Oh, woe," the king said, "beset by all manner of calamities."

"Fear not, O brave—" Wanda was saying.

I fixed the translator again.

"Old Lund kid can handle it," she concluded. "Don't sweat it, monarch."

I turned to them.

"I'm going up for a spin," I said.

"Spin?" the king said.

"You're leaving me here all alone?" Wanda protested.

"I'll be right back," I said. "You've got *him* here. Keep him company."

"Spin?" the king said. "Going up?"

I levitated.

"Talk about enchantments," the king said, and fainted.

The two down below were swallowed by darkness. I was alone, climbing higher and higher toward the sky. I went a long way up. There seemed to be no end to the barrier. It climbed with me. After a while I gave up trying to reach over it. There was, obviously, nothing in that. I changed directions and took a sideways course. This horizontal drive began to take me in a slow, wide curve. The barrier was circular. I opened the levitator wide and, keeping a hand on the invisible obstruction, carved a zero through the night.

It was about a three-mile trip.

And so, now I knew—

Unless I had missed some doorway, this barrier was just plain solid. You couldn't go over it and you couldn't go through it. I wasn't about to begin digging to see if I could go under it. That left only one remedy: the last resort. It was an extreme act—authorized for use only in emergencies—but this would have to figure as an emergency. It was either that or give up the job.

I came down next to Wanda and the king.

"Jeez," Wanda said, "I thought you'd done a back door fade for sure."

The king said: "How do we know you're not the devil? All this you do smacks of the devil's work! Give us a sign."

"Kingy," I said, "you'll just have to take my word for it." To Wanda I said, "We're going to crack this barrier thing." To the king I said, "Sire, it's been dandy. We've gotta blow now."

"Blow?"

"But we'll do our best to get you off the hook."

"Hook? We?"

"Your difficulties. Wanda and I."

The girl brushed a tear from her eye. "I knew you wouldn't leave me behind. You're an all-right joe, Lund kid."

This was some translator I had.

"Blow?" the king said.

"Depart," I explained.

"Where to?" he asked.

"The other side of the barrier."

"But how?" he asked.

"Yeah," Wanda said, "but how?"

"You won't feel a thing, honey," I said.

I reached into my traveling bag and pulled out the small black cube.

"And what does that thing do?" Wanda asked.

"It turns off reality," I said.

"It does *what*, Lund kid?"

I flipped a dial and reality turned off.

I had five minutes.

The scene before me was frozen. Dead.

The girl and the man, immobile. They had become statues, along with everything else. There was no life here; there was absolutely nothing. The lights from the stars were out. No sounds could be heard. The night had vanished. There was only gray now—over everything. A gray, endless expanse.

In this state, nothing could be damaged or destroyed—but objects could be moved like chess pieces on a wide board.

I walked toward Wanda through the gray ether.

This stopping of reality was nothing to play around with, I knew; it could shred reality to bits. Do it once too often and no one would be able to put the pieces together. But an emergency is an emergency. And in my book, not being able to do your job comes under that heading. There'd be some wrangling when I got back to the office, but that was part of the job too. You took the good with the bad.

You did what you had to if you were a caseworker, and you didn't always follow the rules. Sometimes you even made up a few new ones as you went along. The galaxies were a big place. No two were alike. You couldn't play it straight even if you wanted to. You played by ear and were glad when the notes made some kind of sense.

You're Lund and you're a caseworker, and all you know is your job, and if you've got to cut some corners to get it done, that's all right too.

You're Lund and you've been to a thousand cockeyed worlds, and you've seen and felt and done more things than is good for a man.

And, by this time, if you can't spot an emergency, brother, no one can.

I lifted Wanda under my arm and walked through the barrier.

The Tsaddik Himself: Three

It was too quiet.

I ran down the main street.

Gevald, I thought, it's all over, finished . . . the shtetl is *oysgerinen, nebech.* . . .

Turn your back for five minutes and look what happens.

The buildings were all there:

Some, glass. Others, stone. A few, steel, concrete, brick. One was red plastic; two, illydeum from a far sub-line. The model shtetl was there too, in the square next to the garden. . . .

But where were the people?

I stopped in the center of town, looking in all directions. So *nu?*

The movable sidewalk moved. Colored lights from the glass skyscraper lit the magno-lifts, lit the fountain in the square. Two hover crafts hovered.

Only there were no people. What's a shtetl without people?

Greenberg sighed. "Bossnik," he said, "you know what this means?"

"Wiped out!" I moaned.

He nodded his head sadly. "A black day for homunculi."

"Homunculi?"

"Think of all my cousins, aunts, uncles . . . all gone. There isn't a homunculus in sight. Maybe you can spot one; you got better eyes."

"THERE AREN'T ANY PEOPLE EITHER!" I screamed.

"People . . . ? Say, you're right. I hadn't noticed. No people. Some how-do-you-do. Some disaster. On this black, black day when the proud homunculi expire, people, too, turn up their heels. You think, maybe, it's a coincidence? To me, it smells like a plot."

"I like the plot idea myself," I said. "I'll think about it. But, first I think I'll have a grade-A fit."

"A plot against homunculi—what else? With people caught in the middle. Someone must have been jealous. There's a lot of jealousy in the world these days. But, who?"

"Insects," I said, "ants, spiders, flies."

"Don't be bitter, bossnik. Homunculi are rare—where can you find a spare homunculus? Only in stories, poems, selected short subjects. Some sub-lines, maybe. How many? A handful, that's all. This, what's happened, is a terrible blow for all homunculi; homunculi are irreplaceable. But people? With people, it's something else. People are a dime a dozen. Whoever heard of a people shortage? Modern know-how can fill this shtetl with people in no time. Advertise a little; put an ad in local papers. There'll be no end of people. After all, a modern shtetl: hot and cold running water, short working hours, self-service kitchens. That's pretty good for the fifteenth century. You can hardly find it anywhere these days. It's a bargain. Cheer up, boss; remember, it could always be worse—and probably will. You know—whatever got hold of the folks here missed you and me, but now that we're back—who knows?—maybe the mistake will be fixed. Remind me to take a day off if we get through the next couple hours; all this is going to be too much for me—"

Something that looked like Mendel the Teacher came out of the bookstore down the block and started walking in the other direction.

I yelled his name.

"Yoo hoo!" Greenberg called.

That got him; he turned, looked at us, waved a hand and waited.

I wasted no time; I ran up to him in a hurry; Greenberg almost fell from my shoulder. It *was* Mendel!

"Mendel, what happened?" I yelled. "Where is everyone? How were you saved?"

Mendel the Teacher, a tall, broad-shouldered man with a round, jolly face and dark, twinkling eyes, had Susskind the Homunculus on his right shoulder.

Mendel raised a finger. "One: I don't know; two: They went sightseeing. Three: What's this save business? You opening a bank or becoming a missionary?"

"What about the disaster?" I demanded.

"Make a wonder and talk sense," Mendel said.

"So teach me something," I said; "there's no disaster?"

"What disaster? Where disaster?" Mendel said.

Susskind said: "You mean, maybe, in general, Tsaddik, like in philosophy or in particular like in life?" He stroked his long red beard.

I said: "I think I'll go over to the *bes-medresh.*"

"I'm going sightseeing," Mendel said. "Disaster? Things have never been better. Everyone's gone sightseeing. Peace —it's wonderful."

"So now there's peace?" I said.

"Why not? We don't deserve it?"

"We deserve it, but do *they?*"

"They're not here anymore."

"Where are they?"

"They went away."

"All of them?"

"Why not?"

"I'll definitely drop by at the *bes-medresh,*" I said.

We exchanged good-bys and I hurried off.

"So maybe they found a better place," Greenberg said.

"There *is* no better place," I reminded Greenberg.

"Don't be a chauvinist," he said; "a well-traveled man like you, a regular sport—how can you say there's no better place? Sure, we got all the comforts of home; we got no kicks coming, but other places, they got their attractions too."

"For *them*, there's no better place."

"If that's what you meant," Greenberg said, "you might even be right. *Them* are pretty peculiar, when you get right down to it. In fact, I can't think of anything more peculiar, except Muddle, maybe."

"You're pretty peculiar," I told him.

We pulled up in front of the *bes-medresh*.

I pushed open the wide oaken doors and went in.

Courtney: Three

There was no one at the desk in the supply office. Some galactic charts strung out across the walls, a few humanoid journals on a stand, the usual chairs and resters for the waiting throngs. Only no one was thronging at the moment. There aren't that many humies in the Outer Galaxies to begin with—most of the humie density occurs near the center of the Middle Galaxies, a different department entirely—so the place was usually, if not always, pretty calm. Right now it was dead.

"Anybody home?"

"Get out! We won't be needing any today," a scratchy voice answered from the next room.

That would be Doc Scrudge. I joined him.

"Where is everyone?" I asked.

Scrudge was a small, round little humie with a trimmed white beard, rosy complexion and a long, full nose. He lay propped up in a white and tan rester. His eyes were closed.

"Blanket and Middly are on vacation," he murmured, "and so am I—in spirit."

"I got a world cancellation on my hands," I told him.

Doc Scrudge chuckled. "For a second there I thought you said world cancellation." He closed his eyes, went to sleep.

I shook him awake.

Scrudge shakily got to his feet, fumbled in his pocket, produced a small bottle of red pills, popped one in his mouth, swallowed convulsively, then sighed. "Well, here I am. Bright and sober, sport. I hope you're satisfied."

"Sure, I'm overjoyed. It's the job that does it. I love my work."

"Better fill out these forms and stop all these fancy lip movements. Where you bound for?"

I gave him the co-ords.

He shrugged. "I'll look it up in the encyclopedia."

I went back to the outer office, sat down at the desk and started filling out forms in triplicate.

After a while Scrudge called from the other room. "You're going to a world the natives call Gloffnick. Congratulations."

"Gloffnick? What kind of a stupid name is that?"

"You've got me, sport; you think I wrote this book? What seems to be the trouble anyway?"

"A 695B."

"I thought you were kidding."

"They sent Lund down to plug a leak, and he got canceled," I explained.

Doc Scrudge appeared in the doorway dressed in a white smock and carrying a clipboard. "Lund was the short, funny-looking squirt with the big nose—"

"That's *you*," I said, "or Hull. Lund was funny-looking, in a big somber way. I'm finished with these."

Scrudge took the forms, stamped them, returned a copy to me and placed the rest in a folder. "Not a very smart move on this Lund's part, getting canceled. Darkens his record."

"No doubt he's past caring."

We stepped through a side door and into a large storage room. White walls were lined with shelves; the middle of the floor was taken up by cabinets. Odors of canvas, plastic and rubber hung in the air; you could smell oil, gas, turpentine.

Scrudge went to a locker, removed a traveling bag, examined it, gave it to me.

"Here you are, sport, all set, complete except for a couple of small items."

"Such as?"

"No phase dissolver. New shipment hasn't come in yet."

"What about the old ones?"

"You wouldn't want those."

"Look, I'll take an old one."

"Sport, they're just not reliable."

"So what is, these days?"

"Yeah. Only these are more unreliable. As a matter of fact, they break down in mid-phase."

"That's pretty unreliable, by golly; you're right; I wouldn't want one."

"I've got just the thing for you, though. A phase *jumper*; good for a really fast take-off, you know."

"Well-ll, I suppose that's something . . . if they're chasing you."

"Sure."

"Okay, give me a jumper."

"Made by Mangnum and Groper. The best." He handed me a black cube-like device, two inches square, with a dial and two buttons. "There's an instruction voice-slit that goes with it. Here."

I chucked them both into the bag; then I remembered something: "I thought Mangnum and Groper were under suspension for shoddy manufacturing."

"They were. They beat the rap."

"That's just dandy. What other kind of death traps you got for me?"

Scrudge consulted his clipboard. "A levitator," he said.

We walked over to a high shelf and craned our necks. "Up there," Scrudge said.

I lifted a hand, felt around, touched something hard and cube-like. This time it was a red dingus with a green and yellow button. Well, at least there was variety. "This in working order?" I asked.

"Sure, what do you think?"

"You wouldn't want to know," I said. I pressed the green button and slowly rose to the ceiling.

The buttons work the lift-offs and landings; the rest operates on mental control. I hovered for a while. "It seems okay," I called out presently. "How do I get down?"

"Press the yellow button, you fool."

"I did."

"Oh."

Scrudge went over to a pile of junk lying in a corner, found a long pole with a hook on one end, and hauled me down.

"We'll get you another one," he said.

"Forget it," I said.

"You want *this* one? Look here, we can't guarantee there'll always be someone around with a hook to pull you down."

"What I want," I said firmly, "are my retirement papers."

Scrudge chuckled, went away and returned with a different model. "Here you are," he said, "you'll like this one. It's the old reliable kind."

"How old?" I asked.

"It's a Schill make."

"*That* old?"

"Don't fool with the white or yellow buttons! Don't move the dials. *War maneuvers.*"

Boy, how old can you get? I took it up for a spin; it seemed to spin okay. Well, that was something, at least. I landed, zipped up my traveling bag, and got into a clean uniform.

"Going to avenge this Lund guy, huh?" Scrudge asked.

"NOW CUT THAT OUT!" I yelled. "I'm not going to avenge *anyone*. Boy, what kind of stupid nonsense is this? What's all this avenge stuff anyway? All I'm going to do out there is my job, that's all."

I left Scrudge with no regrets and hurried away to blast off.

The Tsaddik Himself: Four

I went straight to the large assembly hall. I pushed aside the heavy plush curtains. *And looked.*

The candle was still there.

Its light fluttered but burned.

It hung in its usual place, in mid-air.

Below it—the large round table with thirty-six chairs. Only nine were filled, and five of the fillers were asleep.

"Hello, Tsaddik," Noodelman said. "Hello, Greenberg."

At least Noodelman was awake. Noodelman would know. He was a long, white beard with bushy eyebrows that had a man behind it. He wore shorts and a sport shirt. Fat Bloom and short Fine were playing chess a few seats away. Krantz, in vest and tie, wasn't even at the table; he was over by the west wall in an easy chair, reading *Der Forverts* by lamplight. The only other light came from the candle. Shadows flickered over the maroon-carpeted floor and ceiling-high bookcases that lined east and west walls. The room was cool, brownish dark, windowless.

"Noodelman," I said. "Am I going crazy, Noodelman?"

Noodelman shrugged. "That smart I'm not."

"Too bad; I'd have liked to know."

"It's always a possibility. You get headaches, stomach cramps; you think, maybe, there's some sort of *imp* on your shoulder—"

"Imp?" Greenberg said.

"—then you're probably normal like everyone else."

"You think so?"

"Of course."

"SO WHAT'S GOING ON?"

Bloom looked up from the chess set. "Not so loud," he said.

"Checkmate in forty-eight," Fine said, starting to laugh for no reason at all.

"Quiet," Krantz said, "I'm reading."

"So *nu?*" I said.

"Imp?" Greenberg said. "Wait till the wee people's union hears about this."

"Well," Noodelman said, addressing me, "that's another question entirely. That question I can answer. On that question I'm the current expert. In this whole place there's no one better qualified to answer that particular question. Which is to say—at the moment—I'm not doing something important . . . playing chess, reading a paper, sleeping. You're lucky you came to me."

"By the way," Greenberg asked, "what's happened to all my relatives?"

"They took the day off," Noodelman said. "Why don't you? Nothing's doing."

"I'll stay awhile. Maybe something nice will happen."

"Nice? You really think so?"

"Probably not," Greenberg said.

"What about my question?" I demanded.

"Question? Ah, *question.*" Noodelman motioned me to a chair. "Relax," he said. I sat down.

"All right," I said.

"Don't worry," he said.

"So who's worried?"

"I'm worried," Greenberg said. "It's my nature."

"Shaddup," I said.

"Our worries are over," Noodelman said.

"Is that so?" I said.

"Sure, it's so. *They* have gone away."

"They have?"
"All of them."
"Every last one of them?"
"Exactly. To the last drop."
"So-o." I thought it over. "It's a trick," I said.

Noodelman flapped a hand. "Why trick? What trick? They're gone and that's all. If you ask me, they went back where they came from."

"It's hot down there," I pointed out.

"They're used to the climate," Noodelman said.

I stroked my chin. "Well-ll . . . it could be . . ."

"Is be," Noodelman said.

"May-be," I said.

"Ech!" Noodelman said. "Why do you always give me such a hard time? Why are you so obstinate? For pity's sake!"

"We Tsaddikim," I pointed out, "are skeptical by nature. It's an honored tradition by us. It goes back to before the change, in fact."

"Us little people are great worriers by nature," Greenberg said. "It goes back to our size. If you were only a few inches big, you'd worry too."

"I worry anyway," I said.

"You're not the only Tsaddik in town," Noodelman said.

"It's true," I acknowledged.

"So if the other Tsaddikim can take this in their stride, so can you."

"I can?"

"Sure."

"Sure," Greenberg said.

"All right," I said. "Maybe I will."

"That's the spirit."

"When did this marvel occur?"

"Some hours ago."

"It manifested itself—?"

"By a vanishing."

"*They* all vanished at once."

"That's it."

"And the whole town instantly left on vacation."

"You're getting the point."

"The town departed for parts unknown."

"You have the right picture."

"Even the little people left."

"An afternoon at the seaside . . . Maybe take in a show later."

"And," I continued, "since *they're* gone, who needs thirty-six at the table."

"You notice," Noodelman said, "the candle stays up."

"I noticed."

"Less output required now."

"I understand."

"We can function with a reduced staff."

"I gathered as much."

"Everything still works, you'll observe."

"I observed."

"So that explains it."

"The mystery's solved," I said.

"It was really simple."

"Child's play."

"And yet you don't look happy."

"It's nothing."

"You're not satisfied."

"It's a small matter."

"Go on, tell me; tell a friend."

"It's hardly worth mentioning . . ." I said.

"Mention anyway."

"Really?"

"Sure."

"All right. I will."

"Go on."

"WHAT IF *THEY* COME BACK?"

"Shhh," Bloom said.

"Shhh," Fine said.

"Should I add my voice to the many?" Greenberg asked.

"Shaddup," I said.

"Why should they come back?" Noodelman demanded.

"Why should they go away?"

"You know," Noodelman said, "that's a good point."

"It's a first-class point."

"It's really some point," Noodelman said.

"You got an answer?"

"Answer, shmanser. We'll worry about it when the time comes."

"Very smart," I said.

"*If* the time comes."

"Incredible," I said.

"We're not babes-in-the-woods. We weren't born yesterday."

"When then?"

"The day before. And if we could live through the change, we'll manage about this, too."

"I hope so," I said, "for my sake."

"Stay in good health," Noodelman said.

"Go in good health," I said.

I went out onto the street.

"What do you think of that?" I asked Greenberg.

"Who knows?" Greenberg said. "It'll be a quiet day here, that's for sure, you mark my words." He vanished.

Alone, I thought; alone in shtetl. Well, I thought, it's been a hard day; lots has happened; there's no denying that! And *they've* gone away. Who can imagine a world without them? Maybe it's all for the best. So what I'll do—I'll go home, fix myself a bite to eat and take it easy. I'll have a normal day. It's been so long without a normal day. Like the model shtetl, it's obsolete. . . .

I got home to my cabin by a tree, on a hill overlooking a valley. Home—it's beautiful. A two-room palace.

I made the spell for food. Nothing fancy, you understand. A chicken leg (hard on the chicken, of course, but what can you do?), a green salad, potatoes and green peas. Some coffee and pie.

There was a terrible crash of thunder; that wasn't part of the spell at all.

Smoke was rising from my kitchen table. Something was standing on it.

"*Oy vey*," I groaned. "A devil."

Courtney: Four

The important thing was to stay alive.

If I couldn't do that, how could I collect my five-rating jump? My vacation with pay? My caseload back at the home office?

The large, wine-colored thing with the yellow spots and the big sharp horn was safely out of the way at the bottom of the well. It was no big trick getting the thing to charge at its own image and land smack in the well. That was, after all, what the image projector was for.

Only now it didn't seem to work anymore.

And that was too bad.

For the huge winged thing with the long saber-like beak and short, stumpy teeth was coming right at me out of the sky. It seemed to be grinning to itself, too.

At the last second I levitated. The thing went sailing past me right into an outcrop of jagged rocks and knocked itself silly. Stupid bird.

Score two for advanced technology and clean living.

That left only the snake to contend with, more or less. At least, I *thought* it was a snake. A foot wide, with a tiny, ugly diamond head on one end and about three yards on the other —that seemed to spell snake, didn't it? Gold, green and yellow scales shimmered and quivered as it crawled. The snake had been stalking me for a good three minutes now; it could sure move. It made me wonder about this place. Whoever heard of a reputable world called Gloffnick, anyway? I could see the snake plain as day from my mid-air perch. It was just on the other side of the hill, cutting a mean streak through the foot-high orange grass. And that was another thing: who'd ever heard of orange grass? Sure, on Kloph 9 and Swivel 2 they had orange grass, but that was because the sky was green and they needed orange for contrast. That was understandable. But this? I distinctly remembered the handbook stating that grass in this region was supposed to be *green.* Or was it blue. Or perhaps brown?

A really interesting thought struck me: maybe they'd gotten my co-ords crossed and sent me off to the wrong world!

That would sure take care of the snake problem—it would be here in just another second, I saw—and the orange grass problem and any other problem that might happen to come along. Because then, of course, I could merely signal for recall. And, by golly, sooner or later I'd be recalled. Sooner, hopefully.

The snake was almost under me, but it was down there, and I was up here. So much for the smart-aleck snake.

Still, there was no doubt about it—the snake had class.

Unlike the wine-colored thing with the horn, the snake hadn't been fooled at all by the image projector. It had kept its beady eye fixed on me from the start.

Eye?

Yes, I realized it had only one large, yellow speckled eye. Somehow that didn't seem quite right either. But then, I hadn't bothered to check the handbook section on snakes. Who would?

I fingered the red button on the levitator. I would disappear over the rise in a blinding burst of speed and let the snake go chase itself. Ha! *Here goes!*

Ho! Here nothing goes!

I was still where I was, and the snake was where it was, looking up at me curiously with its yellow eye. Oh-oh.

I hadn't moved a blessed inch. Some levitator.

A cool breeze was rustling the orange grass. I looked again

and saw that the grass had turned blood red. In the distance dust was rising. Something was coming this way. And fast.

I knew I had to get out before the snake found a ladder or something. Or more company arrived.

I glanced at the levitator and sighed. There was nothing like working with a hundred-year-old levitator, I thought. I was lucky it didn't have a beard on it. I punched the white button. Then the yellow.

There was a stunning lack of progress. Again I hadn't moved.

Then I looked down and saw that the snake had begun floating up toward me. Now that *wasn't* part of the game at all.

It was chuckling to itself, too, I heard—a low, cheerful, contemptuous sound.

Desperately, I grabbed for my jiffy survival handbook. I knew that if I looked long enough I'd come up with something. Probably under "snake."

I glanced at the snake. "Nice kitty," I said. I saw it was opening its huge gaping jaws. Some teeth.

No time for well-meaning science now. No time for anything, in fact.

I punched the green button.

The levitator winked out, and I dropped like a stone.

The snake snapped its teeth at me as I passed by. I slugged it over the noodle with my trusty copy of the jiffy survival handbook. By golly, I knew that stupid book would come in handy for something!

I landed all in a heap. Stars everywhere. For a second, I didn't know where I was. That was nothing new, so it didn't particularly disturb me.

I opened my eyes.

The first thing I did was look around for the snake. There it was, all right, where I had left it. Floating upside down. Its big yellow eye wasn't looking at anything special. I'd apparently conked it a good one.

I tried to move my leg and found that I couldn't: the grass had hold of my ankle. Talk about inimical surroundings! The grass was blood red and dripping now.

The grass looked hungry.

I considered that for about half an instant and then got very busy. I pulled my leg and the grass pulled back. Stubborn grass. I rummaged in my traveling bag, came up with a penknife—and hacked away. The grass swayed and let go almost instantly, after only a partial taste of the blade. Bloody *and* bowed, I thought with some satisfaction. All right.

I knew something now: this was a planet of cowardly grass. But what could I do with knowledge like that?

I hastily inspected my ankle. No signs of punctures, so the blood hadn't been mine after all. Bleeding grass, by golly; now that was a disgusting thought if ever there was one.

I scrambled to my feet, looked around.

There was a clearing—just earth, no vegetation—over by a tree a few yards away. That's where I went.

There was one thing in all this business, I realized, that I had neglected to do and that was partially responsible for my troubles: I had forgotten to consult the voice-slit on the operation of my levitator. Actually, I hadn't had time to—but I should have *made* time. Considering its venerable age, it was, no doubt, quite different from the standard model.

I found the voice-slit in my traveling bag—it was a flat, white, circular object with a sort of mouth at its center—poked it with a finger and heard it go, "Ouch. Honored member of the Cosmos Corps," it said, "the phase jumper in your possession is a Mangnum and Groper product. Feel secure—you can always count on the Mangnum and Groper label as a guarantee of outstanding quality. Yes, Mangnum and Groper is known throughout the galaxies—"

"As crooks," I said.

I shut it off, reached into my bag and pulled out the other voice-slit, the one with the red border. It yelled excitedly: "Schill!"

That was more like it.

It continued: "A name you can rely on. It stands between you and your enemy. On guard at all times—"

Boy, this levitator was really a relic, all right; galaxy wars were obsolete.

"—it takes you up and down, sideways and forward. And, to fool your enemy, we have programmed your Schill levitator with the latest *war maneuvers*. In these troubled times, when a war is liable to happen at any odd moment, nothing feels so good as a Schill in the pocket—"

After a while the voice-slit got down to business:

"Always turn gold dial one-half degree to activate horizontal movement. For full duration or prolonged vertical movement, turn silver dial one whole degree—"

What a nuisance, I thought, but that explained it, sure enough. I had punched the right buttons, but I hadn't turned the right dials for duration. Apparently the levitator *became stationary* after take-off, unless you turned the dials. The dials activated duration. Back at the home office I hadn't taken the stupid thing up long enough to need duration. Now that was simple, wasn't it? Like hell.

I looked around to see what the snake was up to. It seemed to be coming to itself. But who could tell for sure? Maybe it wasn't even a snake. The grass, I saw, had turned orange again. The tree I was near was doing nothing, thankfully, but being tree-like. But the sky was starting to turn black. Now how could that happen? Only a moment before it had been bright as day.

I remembered the dust cloud I'd spotted on the horizon a while back and decided to go up for a bird's-eye view. Reconnaissance never hurt anybody. The levitator, now that I'd acquired the knack, behaved itself respectfully and I shot straight up into the air. The snake eyed me belligerently as I went by, but a caseworker with a functioning levitator, boy, doesn't worry himself about mere snakes.

Below me was a large field of swaying orange grass, a few trees with pink leaves, and small red hills off on the horizon. Over to the right there must have been a blight or something, because that's where the dust was coming from.

There were no towns or villages or anything. I was out in the country, under a darkening sky. And the only life-forms I'd encountered so far had been the things that had tried to get me.

I had been on this world, maybe, fifteen minutes and already I hated it.

Now more was coming (if you could call these new ones life-forms). They were really raising up a storm. I'd never be able to get on with my business if these locals kept getting in my way. There was about half a mile between us. Some were airborne.

I got the levitator moving in the other direction and opened her wide. I could hear the things behind me barking, screaming and shrieking. I got the handbook out, turned to Terra (as we called it) and started looking at representative beings and objects.

What was after me was not a number of pertinent things like chickens, eagles, planes, missiles or anything else that would make sense.

What was after me, according to the simplified handbook drawing, was a herd of:

goblins
witches (broomsticks and all)
devils
imps
and monsters.

Well, that told the story, all right. Now I knew what I was

up against. Except for one small point: the handbook had them all listed under "mythological creatures." According to the handbook, none of these things was supposed to even exist.

I half-turned and peered back. They were gaining on me. How about that? Gaining on a war component levitator! Wait till I got back to the home office and filled out my report. *If* I got back to the home office.

"Go away!" I bellowed at them. "Scat!"

Things became instantly worse. Now that they were certain I'd noticed them, this assortment of horrors redoubled their efforts. They actually picked up speed; their wails, shrieks and howls raced after me.

Boy, what I wouldn't have given for a good old blaster. Of course, that was the one little item—naturally—they hadn't let me take along on this trip. Can you beat that? A bag full of junk and not one blaster anywhere.

The monsters were clear as day now. Talk about gruesome sights. One thing was just a huge, bulging eye with pseudopods growing out of its sides; another looked like a celery stalk with tentacles; giant clumsy creatures that looked as though they'd been stitched together with needle and thread staggered along at a fantastic clip—there was some kind of writing on their foreheads (a brand name, maybe) and the witches—haggy old crones—straddling their broomsticks shot through the air; and devils (quite traditional, too, according to the handbook), horned and tailed, raced along down below and through the skies, trailing streams of flame behind them. The goblins flew on leathery wings and the imps streaked along the ground. There seemed to be some character dressed in a business suit, carrying a briefcase, racing along with this crowd too.

As a matter of fact, now that I looked at them more closely, they didn't seem so gruesome, after all. Some of them even resembled a few of the gang back at the office. Especially that bird with the eye and the pseudopods. Well, it's a small set of galaxies, as they say. But the *aim* of this bunch was unmistakable, by golly; it left nothing to the imagination. You just had to lend an ear to that awful hooting, barking and growling. We caseworkers are trained to catch the subtlest intonations.

The sky was turning as black as a miser's heart. In a minute I wouldn't be able to see where I was going. In fact, that might almost be an improvement.

I considered trying the old image projector (if it was working again) on these jokers, but they were probably too smart to fall for it.

And war maneuvers (whatever that was) wouldn't do much good in the dark. No sir.

There was nothing for it but to unleash the phase jumper. The trouble was I'd be unleashing it on *me*, rather than on *them*. Still, it was my best bet. It would get me out of here, and that seemed to be the most urgent objective. Once I'd shaken these weirdos I'd be able to get on with my job.

I was sorry now I hadn't given a listen to the jumper voice-slit. I didn't know the first thing about this jumper gadget. Well, old Scrudge had said these jumpers were good for a fast take-off, and that sure sounded like the right medicine.

I cast an eye behind me. One glance was all I needed. I dug the jumper out of the traveling bag fast. No doubt about it: they were all but nipping at my heels: wide-eyed, grinning devils; leering, tittering witches. . . . The bunch on the ground was starting to rise into the air, too. It was dark all around now. But the devils lit up the night with their streamers of fire. The racket they were making was enough to burst a stray ear drum. I could smell them, too. Sulphur, tar and the distinct, unmistakable odor of brimstone. Talk about orthodoxy!

By golly, I thought, those finks are getting close enough to start throwing things!

I punched the button and jumped.

Courtney: Five

Boy, Where the hell was I? There was this skinny guy, dressed in a toga or something, waving his arms up at me.

Up?

By golly, I was on a table.

I looked around. No devils. No witches. No monsters. I'd lost them. Well, it just went to show the old jumper was good for something. But what phase was I in? Babylonnese? Greece? Rome? Miltch? Perhaps this wasn't the place that had a Miltch. A lot of places didn't. These things are tough to keep in mind.

The thing to do, I knew, was consult my verifier right away. It would show where I was. First things first.

Only, the guy down below was raising a fearful fuss. Naturally, the natives always want to communicate with us caseworkers. It's unavoidable. You'd imagine they'd be only too happy to leave well enough alone.

I used the translator:

"Pardon me," I said. "I'm a little busy right now. Hang on."

That did the trick all right. His mouth dropped open and he stared at me.

All it takes is the right forceful attitude. Now where was I?

The old verifier.

I got it out of the traveling bag.

Well, how about that?

I stared at it long and hard.

More shoddy merchandise, was that it? Maybe and maybe not.

According to the verifier I hadn't gone anywhere at all. I was still at the same old corner. Co-ords, that is.

Boy, if the verifier was on the blink, I was in the soup.

I looked down at my friend, the native; he was fixing himself something . . . a snack, it seemed. Say, speaking of soup, I was getting pretty hungry. Nothing like a good chase . . . I looked again—he was pulling the stuff out of thin air.

Some native.

He didn't even seem cowed anymore. What was wrong with this native?

It was time to get off the table.

But that, however, was easier said than done. You live and you learn.

There was some kind of invisible wall around the table. Well, there are days like that. Nothing seems to go right. My mother warned me.

Two to one this was the work of the stupid native, I hoped. He looked easier to handle than that other pack. I figured if this was their doing, they'd have shown up by now. Right?

That left my pal.

I knocked on the wall to catch his attention. I caught it.

I used the translator:

"Just what goes on here?" I asked him.

"Huh?"

"You'd better let me out."

"That's what they all say," he said.

"All?"

"All you devils. But, tell me something, just between you and me, how'd you get on this side of the line?"

"Line? Devil? Look, buddy, this is obviously some misunderstanding. Do I look like a devil?"

"What does a devil look like? Like whatever it wants."

"Devils," I pointed out, "do not exist. Besides, there was a whole flock of them after me just a little while ago."

"After you?"

"And there was practically no resemblance between us."

"Maybe you'd better tell me about it," he said. "Come to think of it, you *don't* look like a devil."

"Of course I don't. Maybe you'd better let me off the table."

"Maybe I'd better." *Puff.*

The wall went away.

I climbed down. Well, here I was, but what had happened to the jumper? The last place I was supposed to be was where I was before. I seated myself on a wooden chair. *Puff?*

"Say, how'd you do that?" I asked him.

"A spell, what else?"

"So?" I said. I was getting the idea. It was time for a guess or two. "Magic, huh?"

"This *nudnik* is really a stranger. Of course, magic."

"Everything around here runs on magic, I bet."

"Naturally."

"You make any little side trips . . . ?"

"Like what?"

"Oh . . . forwards, backwards . . . sideways . . ."

"All the time."

"That's what I figured. Where am I?"

"You're in Muddle."

"What's Muddle?"

"What you're in. A town."

"You have a place around here with orange grass that turns red sometimes and that has a lot of spooky beings hanging around?"

The native seemed to go slack. "We got," he said. "Every now and then."

"You wouldn't happen to know how I got here, would you?"

He shrugged. "How should I know. Bus, taxi, rowboat."

"I mean, on your table."

"No idea at all. But you were saying something about . . . devils. Devils are an all-important topic in these parts . . . every now and then. Mostly then, but sometimes now."

"That's very clear," I said. "Okay, I'll fill you in quick like. An exchange of information." I began to—

Halfway through my recital he jumped up. "Pardon me, I'll be right back," and vanished. *Puff* again.

"Hey," I said, "I'm just getting to the good part where I outwit them all. Using modern technology and stalwart courage—" but I was talking to an empty room. I looked under the table, in the closet; I went into the next room and poked under the bed. By George! There was a 3-D viewer on a night stand. I went back to the front room and sat down.

In a very short time there was another puff. He was back.

"Just alerting the council," he said.

"About devils?"

"That's right. Only your arrival seems to have diverted our stock."

"Stock?"

"They stay on one side of the line; we, on the other. They try to cross; we don't let them. The power of the thirty-six keeps them in their place."

"The devils?"

"Sure. Who else?"

"And when I popped up, they took after me?"

He nodded.

"This line you keep fighting over—it's stationary?"

He sighed. "It moves."

"You people," I said, "are in a bad way."

"Look—" the fellow said, "maybe you can tell me something. Who are you, anyway?"

"I am Courtney," I said, "of the Cosmos Corps. A brief sketch of some of our more noteworthy activities will follow."

It followed. These things never take long. There aren't all that many noteworthy activities.

"I see," he said. "Very peculiar. But the One-on-High probably knows what you're up to. I hope. Well, just call me Tsaddik. Everyone does."

The One-on-High? I didn't have the heart to tell him that was Velk the Gazoom. I said, "This is quite a set-up you've got here, Tsaddik."

"You like it?"

"I didn't say that."

"You've looked around? You've seen all the wonders?"

"Well-ll, not really."

"You *haven't?*"

"It isn't necessary."

"It *isn't?*"

"We caseworkers have a nose for wonders. We can smell 'em a mile away. Boy, I'll say. Wonders to a caseworker, you know, are everyday stuff."

"They *are?* Why, I hadn't known that. That's a wonder in itself."

"Precisely. But whenever a caseworker runs into a wonder, right off he thinks of one thing."

"*He does?* What could that be? Divine power? Heavenly intervention? The Supreme Good? Perhaps the multiplicity and diversity of the universe? That's always a satisfying thought. Many think of that. I do myself."

"None of those."

"None? So what's left?"

"Trouble."

"Why, that's *terrible!*"

"Exactly. Trouble usually is."

"BUT WHAT'S WRONG WITH WONDERS?"

"Wonders are *unnatural.*"

"Unnatural? You dare say that about wonders?"

"Sure. Why not? Show me a wonder, and I'll show you something unnatural. Look—by their very definition, wonders are unnatural. In fact, wonders are an awful hazard, an out and out menace."

"*Oy vey,* he's giving me a terrible headache. Why does he go on like this? Make him stop. Why doesn't he stop?"

Very emotional, these beings. I'll make a note of it.

"Well, this must be a real shock to you; sure, I can understand that—but facts are facts. The whole galaxy is in jeopardy. No joke. Wonders will have to cease."

"Ha! Who can cease wonders?"

"Well-ll, when you get right down to it, although modesty almost seals my lips . . . *I* can."

"You? *Nebech ah mishugener.*"

"No kidding."

"*Nu*—if you're such a *makher,* go cease wonders. Go ahead. Be my guest. Imagine—he thinks he's going to cease wonders."

"Okay. Don't say I didn't warn you. If I had time I'd stay awhile and explain. After all, we caseworkers are reasonable chaps. But I'm in a terrible rush just now."

"So, go already."

"Yeah. Bye-bye."

It was *really* time to go.

I pressed the jumper button.

And the scene blacked out. Wham-o!

What I wanted now was to go off somewhere alone and set up my directional finder. By this time, I had a pretty good idea what it would show.

There was a *twang,* like when a rubber band snaps.

It was light again, and I was back in the chair with the Tsaddik.

"Oops. Pardon me," I said.

"I'd just made the spell for a glass of milk," he said. "*You* don't look like a glass of milk."

"I don't even feel like a glass of milk. I was just leaving," I said. "Maybe."

"So good-by."

I used the jumper.

There was that *twang* again, that drop into darkness and the return. Old home week.

"Oh-oh," I said.

"Oh-oh yourself," the Tsaddik said. "Just what seems to be the matter?"

"I seem to be caught in your food spell."

"In my food spell? So get uncaught."

"Yeah," I said. "How?"

"Some ceaser of wonders!"

"Well, Tsaddik, you'll just have to get me out of this, that's all. It would sure save a lot of time, boy, if you got me out of this. Like it's going to be one terrible mess if you don't get me outta this—"

"*Oy*, is this *ah khokhem*. What were you doing inside my food spell in the first place?"

"Look, this in no time for fancy questions. Just do what you have to."

"What I have to do is scream for help. Look, you sure you're in my food spell?"

"Sure, I'm sure. Unless the stupid jumper's really laid an egg this time. The verifier and the jumper couldn't *both* be wrong, could they? Don't answer that."

"I wouldn't know," the Tsaddik said, with some dignity. "But if you're really caught in my food spell, you should know a few things. You don't belong there . . . I don't know how you got there . . . and it may take weeks to get you out."

"I don't have weeks."

"Or months."

"That's even worse. By that time it will all be academic. We've got to do something."

"This will destroy my schedule."

"It'll destroy more than that."

I thought it over. I could always stop reality, but what good would *that* do? The jumper turns off with everything else. And I'd never make it out of the spell on foot. Not in five minutes, I wouldn't. And if I made a habit of using the old stopper, I'd finish off this galaxy before the leak got around to it.

Well, that took care of all my snappy choices. There was only one thing left to do. I had to convince this Tsaddik guy that I knew what I was talking about. The way things stood now, I couldn't get along without him. I needed him by my side.

I sat back in the chair, crossed my legs, made myself comfortable and started to explain.

"Listen," I said, "you'll learn something."

The Tsaddik sighed. "This is all very unorthodox," he said.

"You ain't heard nothin' yet," I said. "First off, I presume you got a truth spell handy, right?"

"Of course."

"Okay. Work a truth spell, so you know I'm telling the truth."

"If you say so."

"Well—?"

"It's worked already."

"Oh. What happens if I tell a lie?"

"A bell rings."

"That's all?"

"How about a hammer over the head?"

"Forget it. Now, let's start at the middle; there's no time for fancy beginnings. You know about the galaxy, of course; you've been around, right? Right." I snapped on the image projector. "That's the galaxy. *Your* galaxy. Lemme show you some others." I went through a string of G's. "That's something, huh? Well, I'll tell you—they all work different-like; it's a fact. You hear any bells? Right! There are millions of inhabited planets." I showed him a couple. Flick! Flick! Flick! No time for tricky in-depth analyses. "More than you can shake a stick at, right? Right. Okay. Just wait till you get a gander at some of the creatures that inhabit those worlds. Boy!" I showed him a couple. "As you can see, they come in all shapes and sizes. Some are pretty cute, too, and some ain't so cute. It's all a matter of taste, of course, but, when you've been bumming around these galaxies as long as I have, boy, you get used to anything. Almost. Now hear this: all planets operate according to natural law. It's self-evident. Right? But —no two natural laws are quite alike. How could they be? Just look at all the different types of beings they've got to accommodate. Sure, magic works in some places; magic is natural law in some places. But with restraints. Safeguards. Within boundaries. Otherwise you'd have—what? Chaos! You may already have noticed some on these little trips you take. Little things going wrong . . . ."

"Like going third person . . . ?"

"Sure. Whatever that is."

"Or the end of the world?"

"Yep, that would count as little things going wrong. You see, on this world, Tsaddik, magic in large doses is strictly taboo. This world was never meant for magic. Believe me. On *this* world magic runs contrary to natural law. Now, the intra-galactic articles of conservation require a 3.2 life survival factor, and you folks have just nose-dived below that. Way below. Well, I'll come clean with you. Actually, we sent a guy down here to fix things and his presence made things worse. An accident. But what can you do? This galaxy, Tsaddik, is going to blow up unless we get busy right now. But don't worry. I'm here and I can handle the job—"

The bell started to ring.

"Maybe," I added.

The bell stopped.

"Just testing," I said. I got my traveling bag open. "Now let's see about this leak, huh?" I was reaching for my directional finder when a beeping noise hit me. By golly—the message receiver. And coming from this world, too. But who could it possibly be?

The Lund Casebook: Three

I put the babe down, gave a look-see. There was still a minute to go on the freeze. Old Casy was on the other side of the barrier looking, for all the world, like one of the permanent fixtures. Okay, Lund, you're back in the thick of things, I thought; let's see you wrap this caper up and tie a bow around it. You've already burned up too much time. These big productions take something out of a man. Yeah—vacation time, that's what they take out of a man . . . not to mention vitamins and minerals lost. . . .

The freeze came undone.

"Oo-me-gosh!" Wanda cried. "Look at that; I'm sprawled on the ground. I'll never touch another drop. Jeez, I've had the strangest weird-o nightmare. Where am I?"

"On the wrong side of the barrier, sweetheart," I said.

"Eeek! It's for real!"

I extended a hand, helped her up.

"Wow," she said, straightening her dress, "for a second there I figured I had just gone *berserk* like ordinary folks. I forgot I'm a princess. Everything's got to happen with a vengeance."

"Can it, sweetheart; we got work to do." I looked across the barrier. The king was gone; he'd taken off the first chance he'd got. That was a smart king for you. A monarch like that might get to go places. Like far away.

I turned back to our immediate surroundings, let my eyes caress the terrain.

The moon was out now, and I could see a forest stretching

off into the night. It was too dark to tell, but it seemed to have a funny kind of color. Red, maybe?

Wanda said: "This place gives me the creeps, Lund kid."

"Yeah," I said. I wasn't going to argue. There was something wrong here; a subtle something. But what?

"It's too quiet," Wanda said.

"Quiet?"

"Listen," she said.

There was nothing to hear.

"There are no crickets," Wanda said. "As a matter of fact, there are no nothing."

"There are know-nothings in every age," I pointed out, "men of small minds and bigoted natures."

"There's not one blessed sound," the girl said, "except us yakking away."

I shut my mouth.

Silence.

I cleared my throat. "It's not supposed to be that way, huh?"

"Only when you go deaf."

"Yeah," I said. I had figured, maybe, this cricket business was a regional matter. How was I to know crickets were part of this scene too? Now the silence hung in the dark night sky like a threatening hand.

"We'll get the verifier out," I whispered, unzipping my traveling bag, "and be on our way."

"Just make it snappy, Lund kid," Wanda said, huddling against me. "This here territory is *eerie*."

What could you expect from a barrier, I thought. Almost anything. Artificial, I thought. That was the word. Somehow, this place was artificial. But did that mean man-made?

I got my answer much sooner than I expected. Or wanted.

Wanda screamed. All at once the place lit up like a fireworks festival.

I whirled, craned my neck skyward, stared at what I saw.

Well—there are legends and there are legends. And up there, in the now bright sky, was an honest-to-goodness legend looking us square in the eye. "The ungodly hosts," as King Casy had so well put it. There they were. In the flesh (if they had any). They just hung there in the sky, a frozen tableau, glaring at us.

It was getting hard to breathe all of a sudden. Wanda had me in a stranglehold. I pried her arm loose with some effort.

"Devils," she hissed through chattering teeth. "Witches. Goblins."

I could see what she meant.

This would take some figuring out.

The tableau seemed to come apart, to fragment. Flame sprouted from the ground around us. The night was filled with billowing laughter. The creatures of darkness were plummeting down.

Well—what could they do, after all? Roast us? Eat us?

Come to think of it, there had been a few nasty cases of that type reported on the more primitive planets. And *this* planet was beginning to seem as primitive as all get out.

Wanda was screaming up a storm beside me. There was no time for reassuring words. My hand had already been in the open traveling bag groping around for the verifier. Now I simply clamped down on the phase dissolver and twisted a dial.

The dissolver did its stuff.

We dissolved out of this reality.

And into another.

The riot was apparently in full swing.

It was bright day.

Swords and spears were flying all around us. Rocks too. The warrior types—the local constabulary, no doubt—had swords, shields and breastplates. The other faction, bearded and tunicked, made do with whatever came to hand.

This place appeared to be a village of some sort, set on a hill; a road could be seen winding away into the distance.

Wanda tried to crawl into my pocket.

I grabbed her arm and propelled us both toward the safety of a small mud hut. We huddled against an outside wall.

"You sure do manage to land in fascinating surroundings, Lund kid," she said.

"Does this place look familiar?" I asked anxiously. The dissolver shouldn't have taken us too far away.

"Yep," she said.

I managed a grin.

"I once had this terrible nightmare," she said. "You see—"

I lost the grin. "More real than that, baby!"

"More real. Forget it. For my money, this is wayoutsville."

I grabbed hold of a small brown-robed, black-bearded gent as he came dashing by.

"Pardon me, friend," I said.

"Huh?" He turned large brown eyes on us.

"What's going on?" I asked.

"I say, old chap," he said, "I'm in a bit of a hurry right now. We're having a riot here, as you can see, and, if we don't do our bit, it really won't amount to much. A shoddy show."

"A shoddy show?" Wanda said.

"It's the translator," I said. "I've got it tuned to super-vernacular."

"I'd never have guessed," she said.

"It's been jolly meeting you," the little man said, starting to take off for the action.

"Hold it, Mac," I said, latching on to a sleeve, "just a word before you go. What *is* all this messing around?"

The little guy tried to tug away, saw he couldn't, shrugged, sighed and took cover with us against the side of the hut. He said sourly: "You are a persistent one, aren't you?"

"All part of the job, brother."

"I dare say . . . some sort of an outlander, aren't you," he said, running his eyes over my uniform. "And, judging by your poor manners, I'd venture you're one of those nasty prying scribes—represent some scandal parchment, no doubt. Out for a swoop, ha?"

"Scoop," I said.

He shook his head. "Around here, it's swoop. Things have been moving so fast it's all we have time for."

"Just where is here?"

"Modin."

I asked Wanda, "Mean anything to you?"

"It don't sound Polish," she said.

"Is it Polish?" I asked the little man.

"What's Polish?" he asked.

"She is," I said.

"It's a country," Wanda said.

"Polish?"

"Poland," she said.

"It seems unlikely."

"Say, Lund kid, what gives with this translator gizmo, anyway?"

"I've never heard of Poland," the little man said.

"The brass likes us to keep tuned to the public wave length," I told the girl. "It makes things smoother. The plain, unaffected, simple, sub-standard colorful speech of the boobs. Sure, the academies might frown on it, but we don't get to interview an academy very often. You dig?"

"I wouldn't dare not to, Lund kid-o."

"I say," the little man said, "but you two are really developing into an awful nuisance."

"Sorry about that," I said. "Just give us the scorecard on all this ruckus and you can trot along."

"Well, you see those chaps over there, the ones wearing the Hoplite helmets and carrying those sharp two-edged xiphos, those are the bad chaps. I happen to be one of the good chaps. Antiochus Epiphanes sent those bad chaps around to inflict all sorts of *terrible* abominations on us. Now there are those who can take an abomination or leave it, and we good chaps prefer to leave it. You see?"

"No," I said.

A spear landed in the wall a few feet from us; the little guy pulled loose and ran away to join the fun.

"If this place is Poland," Wanda said, "it must be a real backwoods section—them guys dress so funny."

A sliver of smoke began to twist in the air. The sliver became a column. The column became a blast of flame.

A pointy-tongued, red-faced, sharp-horned fellow stuck his head through the flames and looked around eagerly.

"Hey, Lund kid—you see what I see?"

I saw. I used the dissolver.

The fortress was plainly under siege.

We were down below with the troops, the fortress high above us on top of an almost unreachable rock. Two paths led up to it; one, from the east rising out of the water below; the other, from the west. Both were treacherous. High, wide walls enclosed the fortress.

There was no sight of our devilish friends. A hot, burning sun glared down above us.

Wanda said, "This beats everything."

It was true; we did look a bit out of place. A milling crowd of men was already forming around us.

"This doesn't seem too likely a spot to set up my gear," I told the girl.

"This don't seem too likely a spot for anything, except maybe a lynching, like ours."

"It's probably great for the siege season," I pointed out. "If you go for that stuff."

A strapping six-footer stepped up to us. "It's obvious, buddy," he addressed me, "that you must be one of the legionnaires."

"I must?"

"Sure. Because no one else could get in here alive. That figures, right?"

"Right," I said.

"That, buddy, leaves only a few small points to clear up. Like where is your trusty *gladius* with which to cut up the enemy?"

"The enemy?" I said. "I don't have an enemy in the world, feller. And I'm not really much of a cut-up. Actually, I prefer the quiet life."

"Sure you do. Don't we all, buddy? But life's that way, ain't it? Hard. Still, we try to make it a little more beautiful by wearing our pretty *crista* on our helmets." He pointed to some fancy plumage growing out of his helmet. The crowd around us was still thickening. "Where's your *crista?*" he asked. "Come to think of it, where's your helmet? And the rest of your uniform. And who's she?"

"That's Wanda," I said.

"Yep, that's me," Wanda said.

"We've got to be going now," I said.

"Wanna bet, buddy?"

"Well—what are the odds? And, by the way, what's that thing up there?"

"On top of the rock?"

"Yeah."

"That's Masada. We're besieging it."

I shrugged.

A puff of smoke appeared over the man's shoulder. A bright red face peered out from the smoke, examined the crowd.

The face noticed Wanda and me. Wanda said: "Shrug again, Lund kid; maybe it'll go away."

"Shrugging's got nothing to do with it," I said.

"What does?"

"I wish I knew."

"Consider yourselves under arrest," the big guy said. "You spies are getting dumber every day. Imagine, tryin' to infiltrate in a screwy getup like that."

"That's nothing compared with what's over your left shoulder," I told the guy. He turned to look.

I dissolved the scene.

The gray ether enveloped us for an instant, then we emerged.

Wanda looked around quickly and shuddered. She clutched my arm. "Jeez," she said, "this takes the cake. Now you've *really* gone and done it. Gee-whiz, you've landed us right in *Hell!* Me-god, this is the worst place ever. Nothing compares to this for ugliness, for awfulness, for terribleness; this has just got to be Hell. Hell, of all places! How did you ever manage to swing it, Lund kid?"

"Talent," I told her, taking in the layout. "This may not be so bad as it looks."

"It's probably worse!"

"Keep cool," I advised. At least, no one was giving us the eye. As a matter of fact, we were being ignored.

Huge crowds poured by us; the crush was something to see.

The air was thick with smoke; large buildings were on one side of us; a campus of some sort, on the other. A strip with speeding vehicles running down its center was in the middle. The noise was incredible.

It didn't take me long to figure out why we weren't pulling our share of attention. The style here was a hodgepodge of costumes: the inhabitants of this place—whatever it was—liked to dress it up. Wanda and I were just part of the crowd.

"This may be okay," I said, "yeah."

"I'll never believe it," Wanda said.

There were signs all over the joint. They meant nothing to me. The weird strokes and lines were so much mumbo jumbo. But I could fix that. I needed a clue to our whereabouts. I got the reader out of the traveling bag and flashed it at a sign: "Chock full o' Nuts." Now what was that? I tried another. "Coca-Cola." Nothing else—just that one inexplicable word. There was no hint how this Coca-Cola was used, what it was for. Maybe it was a person? I had no time to bother with it. Every society has its riddles. But we caseworkers have learned it's better to let them lie. The natives don't often go for strangers poking around under their rugs.

I tried another sign:

"Broadway." Nothing in that. Again, "116 Street." Another blank. Then, "Columbia University." Well, that made some sense: a hall of learning, an isle of decorum and propriety in the very heart of all this bustle. But there wasn't a thing in it for me.

I turned to Wanda. "This isn't Hell," I told her. "It just looks like it. This appears to be a sort of advanced society."

"Advanced? You've got to be kidding."

"Scout's honor. See for yourself. All these tall structures bespeak an advanced society; notice the smoke, noise and dirt; see the glassy-eyed people; observe the traffic tie-up right over there. How advanced can you get, sweetheart?"

"How do I get back to the old castle?"

"Hold on; we won't be here long."

I used the reader again:

"Subway."

Now that was more like it.

"Come on," I said, grabbing Wanda by the hand. We headed for the subway. "It's an underground passage," I explained. "It means sub way as opposed to above way. Overpopulation has probably made these birds build two street levels. We'll be safer down below."

"Down below? That's where they keep the fire and brimstone. That's where they put people in boiling oil. You've got to be crazy to go down below after seeing what they got up above."

This was no time for long-winded, involved arguments;

when you've got a hefty broad by the arm it's best to get moving. I yanked her down a long, dark flight of stairs. A musty odor rose to meet us.

A terrible nerve-shattering roar came from somewhere below. "See? See?" Wanda hollered. "What did I tell you?"

It brought me up short too. But only for an instant.

"Don't let it get you," I told her; "these advanced far-out societies can get pretty noisy."

She began to kick at me with a long, pointy toe. "I'm doing my best not to let it get me. But you're not helping matters any, Lund kid."

I scooped her up in my arms and carried her down the rest of the way. She was saying: "Dragon feed. Dragon feed at my age, and so young and full of promise. At least those German knights ravish a body before doing her in, but what does a dragon know? The trouble with you, Lund kid, is that you're uneducated. Anyone else would know a dragon when he hears one."

We hit the bottom step. I set the girl on her feet. "Look around, beautiful," I said. "See any dragons? Nothing here to frighten a lady but the usual tidbits of high civilization."

"That's scary enough," Wanda said. "This place gives me the willies. It looks like some terrible depressing dungeon—"

"It's probably very advanced in its own way. But we're not planning to camp here, baby. All this fancy maneuvering may have seemed pointless to you but I've got a plan."

"Who hasn't?"

"This one, kid, works. Our tail with the red face seems hung up on one major point—obviously he's got to make visual contact with the pursued. That's us, sweetheart. And us being down on this second level and him being a stranger (I hope) will give us the edge in shaking him."

"What happens when you shake him—money falls from his nose?"

"Losing him."

"Oh. What happens then?"

"We go after this leak. What else? Let's take a stroll, sweetheart."

I figured this underground level was made for walking. Turnstiles were malfunctioning (a sad comment on this place)—I couldn't get them to budge, so we used a door over by the side that led onto what I took to be the main promenade—only it wasn't. This area stopped short at both ends. Tracks at a lower level led into a dark dismal tunnel.

The painstaking caseworker training, that lets us spot cultural configurations at a glance, was at work again:

This was some kind of layout for motorized vehicles. Obviously not for people. Even a short-term visitor like me could see that. This place was too dismal for people. They probably hauled garbage through these tunnels. People would hate it here.

A little man had run out of a booth on the other side of the partition and was hurrying toward us, waving his arms. Probably the watchman. Wanda and I went through the door again. We bumped into the little man. "Just checking on the garbage," I said, and started to move on.

"You a wise guy, mister?" he asked.

Well, what the hell—I knew what that meant in the fifteenth century. But here? I told him that my education quotient was no better than average and steered Wanda toward the stairs. The little guy must have been satisfied—he just stood there and looked at us. It was another plus for the translator.

We surfaced on an unchanged scene. No devils, just the benefits of advanced society.

"Look around, sweetheart," I said to the girl. "This is the way your world may look in the future. If there is one. And if this is a major track, of course."

"Of course. What a nut, hah, folks? Well, I can hardly wait—cough, cough."

"It doesn't have to be like this," I said earnestly. "This is just a possibility. It can be different."

"Like what?"

"Under water. All this could be under water. Or burnt, maybe. There's no end to the combinations. Maybe this is the best this world could do?"

"We could do better back in the castle, Lund kid."

"Sure, but what's to a castle? A couple of thousand square yards. But a big world like this, it's probably got plenty of problems."

"This place is just plain uncouth. It looks uncouth; it smells uncouth; it even sounds uncouth. There probably isn't a real princess in sight. Any world that ain't got a real princess running around is bound to be uncouth. It's a law of nature. A princess knows."

I put my arm around her and gave a squeeze. "You're fun-folks," I told her, "but back to business. Notice, we've lost our tail. See, baby, old Lund knows a thing or two, huh?"

She cuffed me in the ribs with an elbow. "You're a cock-eyed wonder, Lund-o-rooney. And, as soon as I wake up from this nightmare, I'll see your name becomes a household word along with vampire, werewolf and housemaid's knee. Only you're queerer."

Just then another roar sounded from the subway enclosure and Wanda tried to climb up my left arm.

I patted her blond head reassuringly.

A skinny fellow with thick glasses said: "She looks like Veronica Lake. Honest, she does. Incredible, especially in that costume."

"Huh?" I said.

"Huh?" Wanda said. "Who's Veronica Lake?"

He was a thirtyish lad in a striped orange and yellow tee shirt, bell-bottom blue jeans and round steel-rimmed spectacles. His nose was long. His face, pale. His hair, black. He spoke: "Foreigners, ha? Don't know Veronica Lake, ha?"

"Hiya," Wanda said.

"No accent, I see."

"We've got to be going," I explained.

"Too bad," he said.

"How come?" Wanda said.

"I have groovy vibes to dispense."

"Is that good?" Wanda asked.

"Sure."

"Like what?"

"I'll tell you," he said. "You being foreigners, it will add to your education. Increase your knowledge. Delight your soul."

"He's some sort of religious nut," I said to Wanda. "Every advanced society has its share of religious nuts. It's a well-known fact."

"You've got me wrong," the fellow said. "That guy over there, now *he's* a religious nut."

He was pointing at a tall white-bearded man in a shabby suit, tight-lipped and bright-eyed, standing in front of Chock full o' Nuts. Poor guy. They probably make him stand there, I thought. Well, at least I knew what the sign meant now. The bearded one was carrying a placard. I used the reader. "It's too late already!" the placard said. I shrugged.

"He thinks he's Moses," the skinny fellow said.

"I know about Moses," Wanda said.

The man over by Chock full o' Nuts glared at us. "WHAT DID YOU SAY ABOUT ME?" he demanded.

"Let's move away," our new friend said anxiously. "It doesn't pay to get him riled up." We moved down the block. The bearded man glared after us. "I am Irving Kittelman," our self-appointed buddy announced.

I said: "They call me Lund."

"I'm Wanda," Wanda said.

"You know," Kittelman said, "I could swear your voices were coming out of that little black box there."

"*This* little black box?" I said.

"Yeah, that little black box."

"A common delusion," I said. "We've got to be going."

"Wait, wait," he said, "give me but a moment; you'll find it worthwhile."

We had begun to walk. "Look around you," he said.

"Say," Wanda said, "don't you have a world to save, Lund kid?"

"Sure," I said, "but what the hell? Maybe this bird's got a point. Let's take a breather. Being a tourist is half the fun. It isn't every day you land one of the locals to guide you around. It's very educational. Besides, sweetheart, this world isn't caving in just quite yet."

"Wanna bet?" Kittelman said. "Look at all the funny-folks we have here." He waved at the passing crowd. "Long-haired students, disaffected whites and disgruntled blacks, mad housewives, blue-and-white-faced collar workers, green-faced businessmen, policemen in pairs, repairmen, teenagers and toddlers, big, small and medium, all shapes and sizes and dispositions, all textures and colors, streaming past the small shops and giant supermarkets of upper Broadway. Traffic is fierce, a jumble of burping motors, blaring horns, groaning engines. We move with the throng. Vendors hawk their wares from sidewalk stands: ties, shirts, fruits, vegetables. Eateries fill the air with noxious odors; trash overflows the sidewalk. Newsstands offer the latest atrocities in black, bold, screaming headlines. My city. Broadway, the loneliest mile in town. Broadway, my beat.

"It is no place for—the loner, my friends. For the spectator. The wanderer, the eternal questor. Here, down these mean streets, a man must go, the solitary wayfarer . . . cast out upon unheeding pavements, the grim byways of dissolution. It is a time for fools and peasants. For naïves.

"Hear my tale—but hark! Those who enter between these gates abandon all hope.

"Just three hours past I steered, steely-nerved, a course

through the high gates of yonder university. The fierce-looking armed guards on either side don't give me a second glance. I don't look like a troublemaker. In fact, I am almost invisible. After all these years I still resemble the average student. Only worse.

"I come to rest on the concrete steps that occupy the high ground mid-campus. I slump down, exhausted, sprawl over the stairs. A handful of others are doing the same.

"Across the campus is the Butler Library, bastion of knowledge. The building abounds in great names, reputations, the masters of antiquity; the names are engraved in the very stone. Homer, Herodotus, Sophocles. Plato. Aristotle. Demosthenes. Cicero. Virgil . . . They are there for inspiration's sake. No one sees them anymore; they go unnoticed. Even freshmen don't care.

"It is too hot to live, too hot to breathe. A girl with olive skin, red shorts, long black hair, goes hurrying by. I watch her. She seems too beautiful for words.

"Depression, deep and unending, engulfs me; I am submerged in total despair.

"I see quite clearly that it is all hopeless. The bad end that people had been predicting for me all along is here right now. This is it! The just reward of misspent days. Life has been going steadily downhill now for thirty-three years.

"Girls, girls converge on the steps in droves. Classes must have just let out. Girls in shorts, in flimsy cotton dresses . . . blondes, brunettes, redheads. Two stone fountains rise out of the steps behind me, spray water noisily. Distant traffic can be heard on both Broadway and Amsterdam Avenue. A drill rattles far away: a building going up or coming down.

"There are girls everywhere. They come by singly, in pairs, in groups.

"The men are there too—never fear. They aren't alone. Oh, no! Each has a girl; they march by in pairs by the tens, hundreds, thousands. Some have two girls or even three.

"A huge ponderous creature, monstrously inflated, a gigantic blown-up belly bobbing over his bursting belt, waddles by; he wears a tiny, dainty beard. A girl clings to his arm. A short balding fellow, with a strained look, races along, a girl on each arm. An athletic type in sweatshirt and shorts dashes down the midway, a chorus of girls hot on his heels. A one-legged beggar hobbles by, girls glued to him right and left. A wheelchair case whirls past, a horde of girls frantically racing after it. Midgets, dwarfs, hunchbacks, catapult by. They're lost in a swirl of girls, girls, girls . . . arms . . . legs . . . torsos. . . ."

"Oh, what a sad story," Wanda said. "It's heartrending."

"I know," Kittelman said, "it's supposed to be."

"It's pitiful," I said.

"Say," Kittelman said, "are you sure your voice isn't coming from that little black box?"

"Positive," I said.

"You poor dear," Wanda said. "What can we do for you?"

"I'm glad you asked that," Kittelman said.

I thought: Lund, you've drawn a blank. Putting in with this joker is for the birds. He has no memorable insights, no illuminating asides. The story he tells is standard stuff on a thousand worlds. Whatever the secret of these messy people and their messy time, this daddy-o won't spill it.

"There is something," Kittelman was saying. "This little thing that you can do for me. It is a matter of small note, and yet—"

A voice from a doorway hooted, "It's Irving the Panhandler!"

"Yeah," another voice said, "with a couple of marks in tow."

The first voice sniggered.

"Say, Lund kid," Wanda said, "what are marks?"

"Suckers, sweetheart."

"Suckers?"

"Lollipops," Irving the Panhandler said.

"We've got to be going," I said.

"No, wait," he said. "Wait, wait, wait. You haven't heard what I want, what I need, what I must have."

"We can imagine," I said.

"We can guess," Wanda said.

"Money," Irving Kittelman said, triumphantly. "You'd never have guessed that! It's the last thing anyone would think, to look at me. But it's true. Money is what I crave. Money. Desperately, ardently, passionately. The buck, boodle, bundle, cabbage, chips, dough, geedus, grease, iron, jack, kale, lump—"

"Lump?" I said.

"Sure. Lump sum. Oday—"

"Oday?" Wanda said.

"Naturally. Roll, scratch, spinach, wad, not to mention shekels, spondulicks, blunt, brass, tin, rhino, lolly—"

"Lolly?" Wanda said.

"Sucker," I said.

"Marks," Kittelman said.

"We're back where we started," I said.

"Not quite," Kittelman said. "Sugar, salt, dosh, oof, mopus, soap, palm oil and, of course, the filthy lucre. In Latin it's called nummi."

"Do we have any?" Wanda asked.

"What would I be doing with stuff like that?" I complained. "I'm Lund the Caseworker. Not Lund the Banker—"

"My case is very needy," Kittelman said. "In fact, my case is empty."

"Your case," I said, "is dismissed."

"My case is broke," he said, "and so am I."

"This," I told Wanda, "is Irving the Panhandler. He does this for a living. Pay no attention. Pay nothing. We've got to be going."

Wanda pulled a ring off her finger. "Take it," she cried.

"Bleeding heart," I growled.

"Is it hot?" Kittelman asked suspiciously.

I didn't bother to reply "only in summer" or "with lots of pepper" or the few dozen other cracks I might have managed. I used the dissolver then and the hell with him—Wanda and I went bye-bye.

Courtney: Six

Boy, oh boy, leave it to old Lund to go off half-cocked on some stupid tangent. And with that woman yet.

Well—he sure made it back to this time slot, or I wouldn't have caught his report.

But how come the home office hadn't received it? This report was days old. And where was the rest of the story? What good's a story without the rest of it? I turned the receiver dial wide open, but that was all, apparently, nothing but static.

The Tsaddik was looking thoughtful. "This must all seem pretty strange to you," I said.

"Actually, if you'll pardon me, I've seen stranger things. My friend Greenberg, for instance, is stranger."

"Greenberg?"

"He's a homunculus."

"Gee, that's tough."

"He doesn't mind."

"Yes," I said. "Well, those are the breaks."

"I noticed something in that report," the Tsaddik said. "Peculiar."

"Oh?"

"Your friend—"

"Lund."

"That's right. Did you hear where he went?"

"Went? All over the blasted map, by golly. That's where he went."

The Tsaddik held up three fingers:

"Modin. Masada. Moses."

"Yes? So? What about it?"

"Our shtetl is called Muddle."

I was beginning to get a bit impatient. "Sure," I said, "and that's a fine name—" If I was going to get this fellow's help, I'd have to humor him.

"They all begin with *M*," he said.

"So they do, by golly. That's quite a coincidence, isn't it?"

The Tsaddik cleared his throat: "I'm afraid your friend is stuck in Jewish history."

"In what?"

"Under *M*. There's a pattern to all this. Anything connected with Muddle has to have a pattern. If you know that, you know what to expect, what to watch for. It's really very simple."

I sat down to think it over.

"Actually," the Tsaddik went on, "er . . . you're probably trapped in Jewish history too."

What can a humie say when he hears a thing like that? Jewish history? What was Jewish history? I thumbed through the guidebook. Jewish history was the history of the Jews. Look under *J*.

"In fact," the Tsaddik was saying, "we're all trapped in Jewish history. Only in Muddle, that's an asset. No one would have it any other way. In Muddle, being trapped in Jewish history is the best thing that could possibly happen. We like it."

Come to think of it, this wasn't so out of line with a cosmic leak situation at that. "Okay, tell me more," I said. "I'm interested."

"It's like this," the Tsaddik said. "When the change came about—"

"What change?" I demanded.

"*The* change. What else? The one based on the mystic teachings of the *Zohar*—"

"When the magic began?" I prompted hopefully.

The Tsaddik nodded.

"Cosmic dribble," I murmured, with a sigh. "That's what it's called, good old cosmic dribble. Well, these things will happen in the best of places. It's really no one's fault; a run in the fabric of the universe and pretty soon things start hopping around all over the place. Absolutely contrary to natural law, of course."

The Tsaddik shrugged. "Whatever it's called, we took advantage of it. Who wouldn't?"

"That's quite understandable."

"Immediately we began our research. We broadened our perspectives; we became educated."

"In time."

"What else? That's what we found it to be, of course. Time. Imagine that. We borrowed a lot of fine ideas, of course."

"Of course."

"As long as it was Jewish history," the Tsaddik said, "we could get around in it."

I turned to *J* in the guidebook. Jews, it said, were ubiquitous. Now all I had to do was look up ubiquitous. Look under *U*.

The Tsaddik was saying, "But it's funny; things have been happening lately; we don't go where we want to; we even, sometimes, become part of the picture."

"Sure," I said, "the fabric's starting to give. Wait a minute. There's something I wanna try out, Tsaddik, old pal." I reached into my traveling bag. Here was my directional finder; now we'd see a thing or two.

I gave it a twist and it started to sing like a chorus of parakeets. Off, vile sound! But there you had it, and, naturally, it figured. By this time, it was no news. We were in the very center of the leak. Leaksville, you might call it.

The Tsaddik said, "It's embarrassing. We sightsee to seek

knowledge. What else? But some knowledge we can do without. When we become part of a picture, or—it should only happen to our enemies—go third person, that's the kind of knowledge we can do without."

"You guys been *studying* time, huh?"

"Naturally. We have historians, sociologists, linguists, not to mention philosophers."

"What you're going to have is all of history sitting in your laps pretty soon." I could see now what had happened to Lund with this *M* business. These characters had worn grooves right through the fabric of the universe. The phase dissolver was just zipping down these grooves, that's all. I explained it to the Tsaddik. As best I could.

"One thing I don't understand," he said when I was done.

"Just one. You're lucky."

"What was Moses doing in that place?"

"That was the crazy fellow, no?"

"You forget the pattern."

"The pattern. Yeah, that's right. The pattern."

"It probably *is* Moses, *nebech,* stuck in that terrible place."

"Yeah, sure. Who's Moses?"

The Tsaddik told me about Moses. Jewish history again but, in this place, wasn't everything?

The Tsaddik said: "Muddle, Modin, Masada: if these are the real thing—and what could be more real than Muddle—then Moses must be real, too. In some way."

"Yes, yes," I said, "but we've got worse problems on our hands than a misplaced person."

"Not just anyone."

"Well, sure—"

"Moses!"

"Yeah—"

"One of our greatest leaders."

"Yeah, yeah, I got it."

"In *that* place."

"It's no good, huh?"

"IT'S A *SHANDEH!*"

"Sure. I don't doubt it—"

"IT'S THE END OF THE WORLD!"

"Now you're talking," I said. "That's just the point I've been trying to get across."

"Well," the Tsaddik said, "we'll have to do something about the world, if there's no way out of it—but we'll have to save Moses too!"

"Sure," I said, "you bet. Save this Moses. Yes sir, I can see that. It'll take a little doing, of course. Now, if we could dig up old Lund, that might help some; he's been there, after all—"

"You couldn't get there?"

"Well, sure, maybe—with a little practice . . . but, when you get right down to it, I'm kind of a stranger in these parts, you know."

"Maybe Greenberg could take us?"

"Greenberg?"

"He's my travel *mavin*. Only he's off today."

"Off where?"

"He took the day off."

"He comes with the magic, huh?"

"We discovered him. You begin by drawing a pentagram—"

"Forget it," I said. "That's just more of the same: cosmic dribble."

"Greenberg is all right. He reads up on all sorts of interesting places, makes the travel arrangements. Greenberg is indispensable."

"We'll have to dispense with him if he isn't here. For the time being. Right?"

"It'll be a hardship."

"Maybe he'll show up?"

"Who can tell?"

"Let's hope so. Meanwhile, on with the show. Boy, we don't have much time left, take it from me. We'd better hustle! Now, since I'm all gummed up in your spell, Tsaddik, old buddy, since I can't, in fact, make a move without you, I'll have to ask you to accompany me. How does that sit with you?"

"Without Greenberg?"

"We'll compensate. I've got some gadgets here that might do the trick."

"Mechanicals are unsafe! Never trust a mechanical!"

"Tsaddik," I said, "I wouldn't give any the time of day ordinarily, but what else have we got? You can work some spells, if you want to. As a matter of fact, you'll probably have to."

"What are we going to do?" the Tsaddik asked doubtfully.

"Now you're with it," I said. "First, we'd better get the layout of some of these possible worlds and see what's cooking. Now, right away, you get a chance to work some spells, Tsaddik. You got any knowledge spells handy?"

"I have all kinds of spells. What's a knowledge spell?"

"A knowledge spell gives people the knowledge of what's happening to them. Like I'm going to pull some people out of these possible future worlds, and that's usually a pretty big shock. Without knowledge of what's happening to them they tend to go crazy. We'll need a talk spell, too."

"That's to make them talk."

"Now you're catching on," I said. "Ready?"

"I suppose so. You know, actually, before taking a big step like this, before changing the world, I should really, I suppose, consult with the council . . . ?"

"Not changing the world, Tsaddik, saving it. There's a world of difference, right? And, take it from me, if it's one thing we don't have time for, boy, it's some wild public meeting. A wrangle like that could last forever; we can't afford the luxury."

I reached into the traveling bag and took out the puller.

"We'll have 'em appear on the table," I said. "If it was good enough for me, it's good enough for them."

"A stage," the Tsaddik nodded.

We moved our chairs back a comfortable distance.

Here I am, I thought, in the middle of nowhere, pulling rabbits out of a hat. I hope. And stuck in a floundering world, no less. A world that's all set to blow any minute. What any reasonable, sensible humie would do in this fix is no question at all. By golly, any reasonable, sensible humie would flip his lid, that's what! Would go simple with sheer panic. But not me. No sir. I just sit here and take it all, like some stupid machine. Talk about being dehumanized! This caseworker racket has finally fried my brains. I wonder if there's any way to retire with dignity at thirty-six?

I looked around. For all intents and purposes, this was just a sparsely furnished log cabin. Well, you had to hand it to this Tsaddik fellow. He was modest, all right. Most folks in his pants would have built some incredible castle with slaves and dancing girls and the whole works. Boy, I'll say! As a matter of fact, I could go for something like that myself. Anyone who'd settle for a log cabin, for research, for study . . . must really be modest. Well, at least this place wouldn't frighten any of our visitors. It'll probably seem just like home to them.

"All set?" I asked the Tsaddik.

"A Tsaddik is always ready."

"That's what I figured," I said.

I used the puller.

"Being a stone," the stone said, "isn't as bad as some objects might expect. Being a stone, in fact, has its many rewards, its advantages. While a stone's existence is, in truth, somewhat circumscribed, there is surely the deep, permanent satisfaction of stoniness to consider. Does a stone grow hungry? Does the trusty stone—backbone of an entire planet, as it were—ever covet his neighbor's wife? A fig on his neighbor's wife! Does a stone make war? Does a stone put on airs? Is a stone ever demanding or irascible? Is a stone ever naughty? While the stone has been described as traveling little, might this not better be put as staying much? What is the worst thing that can happen to a stone? Gravel. A stone can become gravel. But is this truly so great a tragedy—?"

The Tsaddik said: "Excuse me."

"Yes?" the stone said. "We stones are extremely amiable objects. Who's ever heard of a stone complaining? A stone is instantly prepared to excuse, to pardon, to exonerate—"

The stone stopped talking.

"What did you do?" I asked.

"I turned it off," the Tsaddik said. "This must be some mistake."

"Why mistake?"

"You've brought a stone into my house."

"That's right."

"Well, the mistake is an obvious one."

"Hardly," I said, "this stone is a legitimate representative of the ruling body of his world."

"Stones?"

"Just one of the possible futures you haven't got around to, Tsaddik—not part of Jewish history, you know."

"But where are the people?"

"There aren't any."

"No people?"

"No nothing."

"That's terrible."

"Only for people. For people it's a drag. Stones don't mind at all."

"Are you sure?"

"Unless the puller's on the blink, which is always a possibility. We'll see. Let's try again."

The large ape thing took the place of the stone.

The large ape thing flared its nostrils, glowered, scratched itself with a long, hairy hand and said:

"Bananas. Gimme bananas, boss, and a tree to swing from. That's the life, huh? Lotsa little animals figger bein' an ape is lousy; they figure apes ain't got no manners. That's a lotta crap, yeah; lemme put you straight, boss—the best thing ever happened to this world was when it went ape—"

I made it go away. To the Tsaddik I said, "See?"

"That was an ape," he said.

"I hope so," I said. "That's what it said it was, and it looked honest enough."

The Tsaddik sighed. "Another ruler, no doubt, of another possible world?"

"That was the gist of it," I pointed out. "That exonerates the old puller, I bet, ha?"

"Pull some more," he said.

"Sure," I said, "we gotta figure out what future to settle on."

"Why not the main line. That seemed reasonable. Every now and then."

"The main line? Hell, there isn't any. It all depends on where you're standing. You come at this from the angle of Jewish history, Tsaddik, but that ape probably figures he's on the main line. The stone, too."

"Pull some more," the Tsaddik said.

The devil said: "Our triumph was glorious, quite complete and very *evil*—" He was grinning from ear to ear; his teeth, flashing white in a bright red face.

"Stop! Stop! Stop!" the Tsaddik yelled.

The devil was gone.

"Well, sure," I said, "you've got to expect that. Somewhere along the line those guys are going to come out on top. Once you start messing around with magic, anything's liable to happen. On this possible world, these guys get the upper hand. Big deal, it's not the only possibility. Let's try again."

This time there was nothing.

"Oh-oh," I said, "that's pretty bad; in fact, it's the worst yet."

"There's nothing there," the Tsaddik said.

"Let's not even talk about it," I said, using the puller.

The frog said, "So we meet again."

"Eek," the Tsaddik said. "It's the frog."

"Friend of yours?" I inquired.

"After a while," the frog said, "we just felt compelled to take over. You earthlings were really doing such an *ugly* job, you know. Assuming the guise of the harmless frog, we began to infiltrate. There were many weapons at our command; who would ever connect the frog epidemic of 1990 with the dreaded galactic invasion that was to follow? Who would ever think—"

"Enough," the Tsaddik yelled.

I used the puller.

The huge hulk that identified itself as man said, "Ugh." It leered at us. "Kill," it said.

"Make it go away," the Tsaddik said.

He didn't have to ask twice.

"We have never heard of man," the beautiful woman said. "Is it something to eat?"

We didn't waste any time on that one either.

"I'll try again," I said.

"Greenberg!" the Tsaddik shrieked.

"His great-grandson. Naturally, you should expect we'd branch out a bit."

"But the whole world?"

Greenberg's great-grandson shrugged. "Tough noogies," he said.

The Tsaddik clutched his head.

I pulled again.

The Wenzel said: "If there's one thing I can't stand, it's human beings. Show me a human being, and I'll show you a dum-dum. Still, there's one thing to be said for them—they do taste good. Not so good as rats, but better than grass. Much better. I hate to admit it, but I did enjoy eating those human beings. Too bad there're none left—"

"Too bad," the Tsaddik said.

"Too bad," I echoed.

The Wenzel went back to the Wenzel world.

"Looks pretty grim," the Tsaddik acknowledged.

"Things happen when you have a cosmic leak. The best thing to do with a cosmic leak is to plug it."

"I'll help; I'll help," the Tsaddik said. "A Tsaddik who sees with his own eyes is a Tsaddik who knows."

"I never doubted it. But we haven't found what we're looking for yet."

"We haven't?"

"Not by a long shot. These worlds we've seen, they're no good."

"This you don't have to tell me."

"Listen," I said. "We've got to plug 'em up."

"By me, it's all right. Just so you do a good job."

"You talk funny," I pointed out.

"I'm hysterical. My syntax just goes to pieces when I'm hysterical."

"I thought it might be the translator. We call it translator's drift."

"I'm hysterical."

"Well, as long as it's nothing important."

"Wait," he said, "while I make the spell for an aspirin."

The Tsaddik went puff.

"You all set?" I asked.

"I think so."

"Okay," I said.

I used the puller.

This one looked quite normal (for these parts, at least) and began to speak at once.

"When I was a little kid, Papa used to creep into my room on tiptoe . . . in the evening and silently watch me as I sat bent over my desk, oblivious to everything . . . sunk deeply into my reading . . . reading . . . reading, all the time reading. He'd stand there, my papa, his large belly sagging, his heavy mustache bristling, a squat bulky man of sixty in undershirt and stockinged feet, and his face would be all aglow. Time and again, the doctor had warned him to stop drinking. 'Stop drinking, you rotted sop!' the doctor had roared, but Papa never listened; he paid it no mind. After thirty years of steady drinking, Papa didn't have too much mind left. He is the only man I ever knew who looked like a glow worm at fifty. So Papa would creep into my room stealthily . . . and sometimes he would kind of crawl in not so stealthily. Good old Pop. He was so fuddled, he never noticed I was reading comic books all that time. *Superman, The Flash, Tarzan, Captain Marvel, Wonder Woman, Bugs Bunny*—that's what I was reading all the time. I'd read anything I could lay my hands on so long as it had pictures. Pictures, pictures—it had to have pictures; if there was one thing I couldn't stand, it was words without pictures.

"So Papa would stand there beaming, drooling a bit and beaming, or maybe lying on the floor or over the bed . . . in the closet. Who knows? Once he even fell out the window. Good old Pop, we used to have many a laugh at his expense. 'Study! Study!' he'd yell, shaking his fist. You bet. I figured with *that* sort of endorsement, it was the last thing in the world I ought to try. I kept away from it like poison. I was only a little kid, but I wasn't stupid. 'Hard work, son, hard work will make a man of you!' Pop roared. So right away I decided against *that*. 'By the sweat of your brow will you make your mark!' Pop said. I looked at him then. The only mark I could find was the one he made on his head when he fell down the stairs. The mark was still there.

"It didn't take me long to figure out that, with lots of

back-breaking effort, keen application and frugal living, I'd end up like *him*. Now, who would want to do a stupid thing like that?

"Papa had tried clerking, finance, construction and bartending (the last one almost got him) before he stumbled across unemployment. He found, to his surprise, that he rather liked it; it suited him. He stuck with it for the next fifteen years. (It's a good thing the relief people were around, or I might have had to get a job myself.)

"Early in life I made my decision. When Papa threw me out I knew it was time to make my decision. I decided I would *not* try clerking, finance, construction or bartending. I gave unemployment a whirl, but didn't find it to my taste either.

"So I took up the next best thing. I joined the local political club. It gave me a chance to play pool and make money at the same time. I became a public servant.

"'Friends,' I said, 'study! study! The road to success is lined with study.' What? It doesn't make sense, you say? Right! But remember who I was dealing with: illiterates, mindless people. You should get a load of them sometime, in that district . . . I'd have been ashamed to be seen with them if I hadn't needed the money. I could have told them the road was lined with corn meal. It didn't matter what I said. You see, I had the right answers, the answers to the Civil Service exams. Leave it to the club when it comes to public service. That's what matters, you see. So I said, 'Study, study,' and I handed out the answers to the Civil Service exams. I said, 'Look at Abe Lincoln, folks . . . he was humble like you . . . he was ignorant . . . like you, he had no table manners. But he didn't let it get him down. He had a positive attitude about life. Happy Abe! So study, study.' And I gave them more answers to the Civil Service exams.

"It is truly amazing how a humble guy like me, in this great land, can rise from a position of relative obscurity to wild cheering renown in a matter of days. In a matter of days I was arrested. Everyone cheered, the ingrates.

"They gave me six months. I was lucky; it could have been six years.

"There was a big turnout for me when I got out. My district hadn't forgotten me. Half the constituents were now big-shot civil servants, but they hadn't forgotten. After all, who gave them their big break. Who, single-handed, got them high office? So they came together and proved that they remembered me. Only they hoped that no one else did. Ten minutes they gave me to quit the district. We had a little chat together, very briefly. They pointed out they'd break both my feet if I ever showed up again. Also my head. They gave me an on-the-spot demonstration, a sample. It was enough; I got the idea quickly. I took off like a track star. They saw me to the very boundary, right on my heels. I didn't bother saying good-by.

"Well, that was only the start, you might say. Since then, and it wasn't so long ago, I have tried my hand at a number of things but never at clerking, finance, construction or bartending. How do I get by, you ask. That's a good question. I have often asked myself that very same question. I get by, through adroitness, skill and snappy maneuvering. But mostly I get by through begging, wheedling and stealing.

"What does it prove? Who knows? I've got my own problems."

Well, by golly, this one didn't seem so bad. He certainly seemed better than the stone or the frog or the thing that said, "Ugh" and "Kill." "What's your name, kid?" I asked.

"Irving Kittelman."

"Arrggg," the Tsaddik cried, "Irving the Panhandler!"

The Tsaddik Himself: Five

"I'd really like to stay and help out," Irving the Panhandler said. "Honest. No joke. But I've just come into unexpected sudden wealth. This antique was given me. A gift, you might say. A presentation, of sorts. One for valorous—"

"It's the ring," I said. "He's talking about the ring."

"It's the stupid ring she gave him," my new friend Courtney said. "He thinks he's rich now."

"Rich! Rich! And about time, too. Yes, it's not for nothing I've worked, slaved and sweated . . . hey! How did you know that? WHAT'S GOING ON AROUND HERE? You guys know something I should know? The thing's a fake, huh? . . . it's no good, huh? . . . is that it? Come on guys, you can tell me—"

I said, "Maybe he'd like to come off the table. More *heymish*, after all."

"SWINDLED!" Kittelman groaned.

"Hey, buddy, you wanna come off the table?" Courtney asked.

"ROBBED! BILKED! Table? Say, how about that?" Irving the Panhandler climbed down. "Gee, I was up on a table. . . ."

"Have a seat," I said.

"Seat? How much is it worth?"

"Sit down," Courtney said.

Kittelman sat facing us. "It's not right to take advantage of an orphan," he said.

"*Gevald*," I said. To Courtney I said, "Are you *sure* he's an improvement over the stone and frog?"

"Sure? Who's sure of anything?"

"Look here," Kittelman said, "if you want to consult with me, it'll cost you; consultation fees come high these days—"

"That's just it," Courtney said, "you're not in these days anymore."

"You're in those days," I said.

"Those days . . . ?"

"In those days no one's even heard of a consultation fee," I pointed out. "In those days consultation fees were totally unknown."

"How the hell did I get in those days?" Kittelman asked.

"That's some knowledge spell you've got there, Tsaddik, old pal," Courtney said.

"You maybe can do better?" I said.

"How'd you like to save the world?" Courtney asked our guest.

"What's in it for me?"

"You go on living."

Kittelman thought it over. "I could go for something like that."

"I figured you might see the advantages," Courtney said.

"What do I gotta do?"

"How's your history?"

"My history? It's okay, I guess. 'When I was a little kid'—"

"Quiet! We already know that history. Boy, what a one-track mind. Look, I mean world history—"

"Remember," I said, "what we're trapped in."

"Make that Jewish history."

"Sure, I know Jewish history."

"Does he, Tsaddik?"

I made the truth spell. No bells.

"He knows," I said.

"We need a guide through Jewish history," Courtney said.

"Ah!" said Kittelman. "That's me all right. You bet. Faithful, trustworthy, obliging, knowledgeable. Trusty to a fault."

"Wait a minute," I said. "Hold everything. STOP! Him you need as a guide through Jewish history?"

"Sure. You've got a better idea?"

"Yes. ME! The logical choice."

Kittelman said, "Try 'the people's choice'; that one used to work wonders for me."

"I'll work my own wonders, thank you! Look. You go to outsiders, to strangers—when *I'm* here? Is that the way to treat a Tsaddik? Who could be more of an expert on Jewish history than me?"

"Well-ll—there're all kinds of Jewish history—"

"*Oy vey*, what's he saying? What terrible idea is this?"

"No worse than all the other terrible ideas. I'll tell you, Tsaddik, every time track is different. Right? No two histories are alike. We need just *one* history, preferably from an advanced, reasonable society—"

"That's us, all right," Kittelman said.

"—but if we have to, we can drop the 'reasonable'—"

"You'll have to admit we're advanced," Kittelman said.

"But are you best?" I asked.

"They don't have to be best," Courtney said. "According to the galactic handbook, all they've got to be is advanced—"

"We're so advanced it hurts," Kittelman said.

"—who has time to fool around with all this *best* stuff? Who even knows what best *is*? We're in a crisis, boy! I'll say! We gotta move on this thing. Follow the handbook! Follow me, men. Hip, hip, hip . . ."

"I think I'm getting the point," I said.

"Sure," Courtney said. "The trick now is to get the right being in the right place according to this guy's time track. You've visited so many tracks, Tsaddik, that you're overqualified."

"Over-qualified? Already? And so young, *nebech*."

"Well, that's life, baby," Kittelman said. "Over-qualified is something I'll never have to worry about. Everything else yes, but that no. Still, Jewish history is something I know."

"Greenberg should be here," I said, "he really knows."

"So did the Shadow," Kittelman said. "And look what happened to him; he got canceled."

"Please," Courtney said, "don't use that word. Not yet. By golly, we really *do* gotta hustle."

"Wait," I said. "One question. Just one."

"Yeah?"

"What happens to the other time tracks?"

Courtney shrugged. "They fade out after a while or something."

I clutched my head, rocked back and forth and jumped up and down.

"You're trying to tell me something," Courtney said.

"Wait. I haven't begun to wail yet and rend my clothes. That comes in a second."

"Come now—" Courtney said.

"No," I said, "I don't think so. I really don't. I'll be too busy sitting *shivah*. You'll just have to excuse me."

"Excuse you? You've done something bad?"

"Something good. The deal's off. I'm not going."

"Arrggg!"

"I've already used that expression," I pointed out.

"Look," Courtney said. "You don't understand."

"What's to understand?"

"We're all going to be blown up."

"Better that than murder people."

"Since when are stones and frogs people?"

"They're not the only ones."

"And who said anything about murder?"

"Turn it upside down or sideways, it's still murder. I won't do it."

"What I said was fade out *or something.* The important word is *something.*"

"So what's something?"

"How should I know? You think on my salary I've got time to look into all these loose ends? *Something happens.* If it were bad, you think the corps would let it go through? Don't answer that. Just remember: everything comes to an end if we don't start hopping. You, me, Kittelman, everything."

"No, no," Kittelman cried, "I couldn't stand that. The thought's too gruesome."

"Down, boy," Courtney said; to me he said, "It's the way of the galaxies, Tsaddik. There's got to be a main track, you know. By golly, all these other tracks are just symptoms of the leak. They don't belong in the same galaxy with the rest of us. And if we can get this stupid leak plugged, they'll go back to where they came from . . . or something."

"That's all very reassuring—almost," I said.

"Well, yeah, sure. I'm a caseworker, not a philosopher. Philosophers are another department entirely. But you can forget about this murder bit right now. Boy, they don't pay me enough to murder people. Anyway, in the galaxies you can't murder anyone without a license. They'd never stand for it. We caseworkers have our own problems. Now you see?"

"I have a choice?"

"That's the old spirit."

"We get to save the world, ha?" Kittelman asked hopefully.

"Sure," Courtney said. "That's it, all right. That's the name of the game. We get to save the world. You, me and him included. (I hope.)"

The Lund Casebook: Four

Wanda said, "Lund kid, you've got to be kidding."

We were in the gray-in-between.

"Now don't get excited," I said, "I can explain everything. This is the gray-in-between."

"Obviously."

There were only billows of gray cloud in the gray ether. There was nothing else.

"I suppose it takes some getting used to," I admitted.

"Hell, no; my life's been one gay whirl these last few hours. All this gray is very *calming*. It's the hanging upside down that gets me."

"Oh."

I righted the frame on the phase dissolver.

"How's that?" I asked.

"Better."

"It's all a matter of mental orientation," I pointed out. "Actually there is no up or down in the gray-in-between."

"That's just dandy to know, Lund-o-matic; it's so *comforting*. But do we have to keep hanging in mid-air like this?"

"Well-ll, it's all mid-air around here. We *could* pull up a cloud. . . ."

We did. Our feet dangled over the edge. Anything to please a lady.

"Wait till I tell the folks back home about this," Wanda said.

"There won't *be* any folks back home if I don't get busy soon."

"Busy away, Lund kid."

I rummaged in my traveling bag.

"There's really nothing to it," I said. "In fact, I can't understand why I'm having so much trouble. Plugging a leak is the simplest thing in the worlds."

"There're a lot of 'em, huh?"

"Leaks?"

"No. Worlds."

"Sure."

"Maybe this one's different."

I laughed. "It doesn't work like that, sweetie; take it from me, you've seen one, you've seen them all."

I had the finder out now. This time I put it on a narrow "personal" beam. Now we'd see a thing or two. "We'll give it a minute to warm up," I said.

"Pardon me," a voice said.

Wanda said, "Yikes!"

I looked over my shoulder. A head was sticking through the clouds.

"Hi, there," the head said.

"Better forget everything I just told you," I said to Wanda. "This world is a mess!"

A body came with the head. Head and body climbed out of the cloud bank and started over to us.

"This doesn't figure," I said to Wanda. "I expressly picked the gray-in-between because it's mostly impenetrable, inaccessible and out of the way."

"*Was* mostly," Wanda said.

The man sat down next to us.

"You really must forgive me"—he smiled affably—"but I just couldn't *help* following your 'personal' beam."

He was a big fellow with an athletic build, rosy complexion and yellow hair, who carried a briefcase, was dressed in a gray business suit and wore a Homburg hat.

"You're not a devil?" Wanda asked.

"Gracious no," the man beamed, "I'm Myron."

He gave me a card. It read:

MYRON OF THE OUTER REGIONS
REAL ESTATE

"See?" he said.

"I'm beginning to," I admitted. To Wanda I said, "The light begins to dawn." To Myron I said, "The next thing you're going to do, I imagine, is offer me a fortune to lay down on the job, huh?"

"Well-ll . . ." Myron said.

"Wealth beyond my fondest dreams, I suppose."

"Actually things aren't *quite* that fluid. . . ."

"No wealth beyond my fondest dreams . . . ?"

Myron shook his head. "I'm afraid not. Actually the expense account couldn't stand it. How about a six-month paid vacation to the resort area of your choice. Cha! Cha! Cha!"

"Cha, cha, cha? Who needs it? Besides, the corps have a very liberal vacation plan."

"Would a discount certificate to a galactically known haberdasher interest you, perhaps? Fantastic savings!"

"No doubt. Look—how about a little asteroid or something with a modern castle, say, an indoor swimming pool and lots of gorgeous female slavies?"

"Lund kid!"

"Quiet," I told Wanda. "This is men talk."

Myron sighed. "I wish I could," he said. "I really do. I could use something like that myself."

"Say—things *are* pretty tight, aren't they?"

"You'd never believe it. Still, they're bound to pick up sooner or later; sooner for me if I can close this world deal."

"World deal?" Wanda said.

"Yes," I said. "He probably means wiping all living matter off this globe; erasing one complete time track of all inhabitants. Something along those lines, huh, Myron old sport?"

"How about the five-and-dime concession on Glimpk 5, huh?"

"Forget it. It'll take more than that to suborn me, pal."

"I was afraid it might."

"I must have been napping," Wanda said, tugging at my elbow. "Did someone say something about wiping everything out?"

"Yep," I nodded. "That's it, all right."

"Women have no head for business," Myron said. "What do women know of high finance?"

"But *why?*" Wanda asked.

"Why not?" Myron shrugged.

"Resort Area," I said. "There might be an economic crunch right now—true enough. Something of a down trend. A slight depression even—but resort areas always make plenty. The 'people' at Universe End—that's Myron's bunch, sweetie—could really make a killing here."

"I've noticed," Wanda said.

"Economics," Myron said, "will probably always remain a mystery to the fairer sex."

"Myron's 'people,'" I said, "specialize in resort areas. They build 'em everywhere."

"HE'S RESPONSIBLE FOR THIS LEAK THING!" Wanda howled.

"Gracious no, dear lady. That, in fact, is what brought me here. Leak activity. Merely capitalizing on a natural phenomenon. All according to regulations."

"Regulations?"

"The galactic Real Estate Commission," I told her.

"Imagine a galaxy without regulations." Myron shuddered.

"THEN HE'S RESPONSIBLE FOR THE DEVILS! THAT'S EVEN WORSE!"

"Hardly." Myron smiled benignly. "The devils, et al.—those mischievous creatures—were here all along in their respective time track. The leak, one might say, liberated them. I, of course, *did* make *certain* suggestions as to their mode of behavior. . . ."

"You see, sweetheart," I said, "according to regulations he can't lay a finger on this world—"

"Regulations?" Myron fumed. "RED TAPE!"

"—however, a real live autochthon could blow this world to kingdom come."

"It's an autochthon's *right*," Myron said, "if he wants to."

"They don't want to?" I asked in some wonder.

"Oh, I've tried and tried," Myron confided. "The stone people simply gave me the cold shoulder; all the ape thing wanted was bananas; the frogs—if that's what they were—were completely unreasonable: they tried to dissolve me with some sort of ray; the hulk people tried to eat me; the little people ignored me and the Wenzel chased me down a long cobblestone street. I almost broke a leg. We executives aren't used to that kind of treatment."

"The devils weren't any help, huh?"

"You know how devils are," Myron said. "Irresponsible. They like skinning people alive, roasting on the open fire, boiling in tar . . . things of that nature. But when it comes to really big, important things like blowing up a world . . ." he shrugged, "and anyway it's not that easy. For every devil, you know, there seems to be an opposite working against him, something called a Tsaddik."

"A what?" Wanda said.

"Never heard of it," I said.

"And to make matters worse," Myron said, "—you're really not going to believe this—I seem to be stuck in something called Jewish history."

"That *is* rather far-fetched," I said.

"It's unnerving," Myron said.

"Jewish *what?*" Wanda said.

"However," Myron said, "I *am* making progress of a sort. In fact, it's only a matter of time."

"Want to bet?" I said. "Imagine trying to buy me with peanuts. Well, nuts to all that. I'm plugging the leak."

"We'll see about that," said Myron. "I've taken steps." He tipped his hat. And sank through the cloud. Exit Myron.

Wanda looked at me. "By the way, there *is* something I've been meaning to ask you; just how *do* you plug a leak?"

"Nothing to it," I explained. "You're a caseworker, see? and you know your job. You've been to a thousand worlds and righted a thousand wrongs (more or less) and still the jobs keep piling up. It's a good thing you have your galactic handbook or by this time you couldn't spot a right from a wrong if your life depended on it. Anyway, it's all down there in black and white; all you've got to do is follow orders. To plug a leak, sweetheart, you put those beings who've leaked into the wrong time track back into the right one."

"That's all?"

"That's enough. Most of the leakies are usually big shots, honey. History congeals around them, so they're the first to leak through. They all leave a trail a mile wide. You start by locating the major leak areas. That's when the directional finder does its stuff. Then set the finder to 'personal.' Zeroes right in on 'em, you know."

"I didn't know."

"How could you? Of course it's no cinch getting the goods on where some of these birds used to hang their hat. Half the time they don't know themselves. And if you let things slide too long, the time tracks start acting up."

"That's bad, huh?"

"There are worse things," I said, "but offhand I can't think of any."

"Waddya do?"

"Cancel a few, sweetheart. But don't worry. We haven't reached that stage yet. And we won't either. That Myron creep tipped his mitt when he locked in on my finder. He's going to make things easy for us. Some of our leakies must have been sitting right in his lap for him to have caught my beam."

"That's good, huh?"

"For us, baby. All that chit-chat was just a stall. I was getting a fix on him. With my puller."

"Don't tell me, let me guess. It pulls things, huh? It's gonna pull this Myron, right?"

"He's got it coming," I said, "but actually it's going to pull *us* to *him*. And—unless I'm way off base, to our first load of leakies."

"I get it now, Lund kid."

"You do?" I said with some amazement.

I used the puller.

Courtney: Seven

At least we were right in the center of the leak. That was something, anyway. Boy, what a mess this was turning out to be. I got the finder out and flicked it to "personal." This had better work, by golly, it was probably our last chance. Hell, I shouldn't have let them rope me into coming here in the first place; these leak situations can get dangerous.

"Okay, men," I said, with more confidence than I felt, "fall in. Tsaddik, stick close. Kittelman, keep your wits about you. Courtney, take a lunch break—oops, no time. Here goes, guys."

I used the jumper. *Splunk.*

We were in the middle of a huge crowd. In a marketplace, it seemed. An altar was set up near one end and a sacrifice of some sort was in progress. These sacrifices, boy, are the same the galaxies over; all they do is add to the air pollution problem; still, they seem to keep the natives happy; and a happy native is one less headache, as we say in the corps. Good old stupid corps.

The Tsaddik exclaimed, "I know this place!"

"Sure," I said. "Why not? All this traveling around has worn grooves in the Universe fabric, remember? So where are we?"

"Modin!"

"Ah!" Kittelman said.

"Rings a bell, does it?" I inquired.

"Not yet," the Tsaddik said; "he hasn't lied yet."

"I recite," Kittelman said, "from memory, no less: situated upon a hill near Lydda, on the road from Jerusalem to Jaffa stands proud Modin."

"Very poetic," I said, "but what we need is history, not geography. Wrong discipline," I pointed out.

"Let's see," Kittelman said. "You said this would be a major event, a turning point, an occurrence of imposing significance?"

"Yeah. Something like that."

"Modin has always been a very peaceful town," the Tsaddik said. "What could possibly happen?"

"I know!" Kittelman yelled, "I know!"

"Keep it down, buddy," a man standing next to us said. "The king's officers is makin' a sacrifice. We don't wanna get them guys mad at us, now do we?"

"That's it!" Kittelman whispered. "This must be Modin, 166 B.C.! Now get this: the Seleucid king—see?—rules over Palestine. He's just commanded the Jews to worship *pagan* deities. Naturally, they're not going to do *that!* This is a *pagan rite* we're witnessing. And so there's going to be trouble any minute now! You just keep your eyes open, that's all. You're right, of course, this is a truly grandiose chapter in Jewish history: any minute now Mattathias the Priest is going to step out of this crowd and *strike down* that guy offering a sacrifice. And then he's going to *slay* the government agent and pull down the altar. Friends, we're in at the start of the *Maccabean revolt.*"

"Revolt?" the Tsaddik said. "When did they do that?"

I turned to the native who'd addressed us. "Mattathias around here somewhere?" I asked casually.

"Trouble, trouble," Kittelman said, "any minute now terrible trouble."

"Yeah," the native said, "you bet, buddy; he wouldn't miss this for the woild. He's the old party with the long white whiskers over there. The one with the smile on his kisser."

"He's getting set to wreak a *terrible* vengeance," Kittelman said. "Ever hear of Hanukkah, Tsaddik?"

The Tsaddik shook his head. "Is it something to eat?" he asked.

"Come on, guys," I said. "We'd better get moving." Slowly we made our way through the crush. Up on the altar they were busy roasting a goat. I tapped the old, white-bearded gent on the shoulder. "Quite a shindig," I said.

"Oh boy," he said, "there's really nothing quite as tasty as sacrificed goat. We get to eat it, you know."

"Say," Kittelman said, "when're you going to slay that guy up there?"

"I beg your pardon?"

"You'd better hurry," Kittelman said, "the ceremony's almost over."

"Goodness, whatever for?"

"Er . . . you are Mattathias the Priest?"

"Of course."

"And you're not going to slay anyone?"

"Slay someone? How revolting."

"That's it exactly!" Kittelman yelled.

"Hush you!" an old woman snarled. "Respect for a sacrifice!"

"But why should I want to do something naughty like that?" the priest asked.

"Aren't you enraged that they're holding these pagan rites here?"

"Pagan goat is quite mouth-watering, you know. It's one of my favorite dishes, in fact. And with prices what they are it's simply a blessing to get it this way."

"A blessing?" Kittelman groaned. "But what about Hanukkah?"

"Hanukkah? What's that? Something to eat?"

I said, "I take it, sir, you're not too disturbed about all

these goings-on here. These sacrifices. These pagan rites."

Mattathias the Priest shrugged. "Live and let live, I always say."

"But, but, but," Kittelman said sternly.

The white-haired patriarch smiled. "The king, no doubt, means well."

"See?" the Tsaddik said, "it's a very, very peaceful town."

"Only in some time tracks," I pointed out. "It's the right town but obviously the wrong Mattathias."

"Why get upset?" the old man continued. "By all reports, the king, Antiochus Epiphanes, is a man of splendid character."

"Ach! You mean that terrible tyrant?" the Tsaddik now asked wide-eyed.

"Let's get going," I said.

"Who am I to judge?" Mattathias demanded.

I used the jumper. *Splank.*

"Run! Run! Run!" The shrieks came from all sides. We had bought in on something, all right. We were in the middle of a rout.

"Quick, Tsaddik! A protective shield," I called.

The Tsaddik went *puff.* "Consider yourselves protected," he said.

A mighty force was storming down from the fortress on the hill. Around us men were running for their lives.

"We'd better stop one," I said.

The Tsaddik gestured. A small guy leaned an elbow up against our protective shield. "What's up, doc?" He was carrying quill and parchment. He looked an intelligent sort.

I said, "Where are we?"

"That's Masada up there, mate, on that rock."

"Ah!" Kittelman said. "It's all clear now. The doomed fortress Masada. Besieged by the Romans. All Jewish hands lost. A terrible misfortune."

"Lost, my foot!" the little man said. "Here they come now. There won't be a Roman left alive, I tell you, when this is over."

"Good grief!" Kittelman said.

"It's their new leader, that Bar Kochba! He shows no mercy. Oo-o, he's such a meanie!"

"Now wait a minute—" Kittelman said.

"Not that I'm worried, mind you," the little man said. "After all, I'm Jewish myself."

"Yes," the Tsaddik said, "you look sort of Jewish."

"Funny, they usually say I don't."

"But what are you doing here," the Tsaddik asked, "in the Roman camp?"

"Recording history, what else?"

The Tsaddik's face lit up. "Don't tell me you're Josephus—"

"Okay, mate, I won't."

A big guy came running by. "Come on, Josephus," he called to the little man, "we'd better run for it; here they come."

"Excuse me," Josephus said. He trotted off.

"Now hold on," Kittelman said. "That's impossible. Josephus and Bar Kochba weren't even around at the same time. Bar Kochba comes much later, like in 132. He had nothing to do with Masada. It was before his time. Masada was a disaster. A total catastrophe."

"Here we go again," I said, using the jumper. *Splink.*

"No," David said. "I will definitely not play for King Saul. Actually, you know, I've given up music. Haven't played in years." *Spliggg.*

King Solomon made a face. "You really want I should answer a question like *that?* And me with only a grade-school education? Go ask one of my smart aleck ministers. They get paid for answering questions." *Spliddgg.*

"What!" cried Esther. "Marry that drip King Ahasuerus? Why, I'd rather have my head chopped off."

"Yes, my dear," said Mordecai. "You probably will." *Splunkell.*

"Actually," said the great scholar Jachana ben Zakkai, "when you come right down to it, I'd rather *not* found an academy. Life's short; let's live it up." *Spliggell.*

"You know what?" said Ezra.

"No, what?" asked Nehemiah.

"Why go to Jerusalem when we can stay here in nifty Persia?"

"Why, what a splendid thought," Nehemiah said. "But aren't we supposed to canonize the five books of Moses there?"

"Aw, let someone else handle that." *Splup.*

"A Jewish state in Palestine?" chuckled Theodor Herzl. "You must be kidding. That's the most ridiculous idea I ever heard. . . ." *Sppplllungputputput.*

"STOP!" said the Tsaddik. "Wait till I make the spell for aspirin."

I said, "Where are we now?"

"You're asking *me?*" moaned Kittelman. "It's quite obvious, I don't know *anything.*"

"I know," the Tsaddik said.

"Yeah?" I said.

"Egypt," said the Tsaddik.

Kittelman wiped his brow. "Moses, huh?"

"Don't worry," the Tsaddik said. "He won't be here. And if he is, he'll love it here in Egypt. Deserts will be the one thing he's allergic to. Probably he'll be a slave-master. And an atheist. Who knows, he may even be married to royalty? Here Moses is probably the Pharaoh."

I said: "Boy . . ."

"There's the Nile," the Tsaddik said.

"—wrong each time," I said.

"That's the Temple of Amūn," the Tsaddik said.

"We must have set some record," I said. "It just isn't natural, by golly, to miss each time."

"Greenberg took me on a tour here recently," the Tsaddik said. "Soon we'll come to the slaves."

"Against all odds, in fact . . ." I said. "Maybe we'd better ask for this Moses fellow."

We were walking by the side of a lake. The Tsaddik went over to a man sitting by its banks. "Is there a Moses around here somewhere?"

"You mean Moses the turncoat?" the man asked.

"Never mind," the Tsaddik said.

We kept on strolling. "*Nu?*" the Tsaddik said.

"*Nu?*" I said.

"*Nu?*" Kittelman said.

"You hear something?" the Tsaddik said.

"Like what?" Kittelman asked.

"Footsteps. Giant footsteps."

I looked around. "Yeah," I said. "I seem to hear something like that."

"Oh-oh," the Tsaddik said.

"What's up?" Kittelman said.

"I just remembered," the Tsaddik said.

"Well?" I said.

"We're stepping," the Tsaddik said.

"Yes?" I said.

"—where we shouldn't."

"Gee, you sound funny," Kittelman said.

"I'm hysterical," the Tsaddik said. "That's all."

"Just what's wrong?" I asked.

The Tsaddik said, "That building we passed a little while ago. Remember that building? That's where the war god Montu lives—"

"So?" Kittelman asked.

"He don't like we should step on his ground. Sacred, you know."

"And we are—" I said.

The Tsaddik nodded. "Stepping on his ground."

"So what?" Kittelman said. "Big deal."

"You said it," the Tsaddik said. "Very big."

A huge figure had appeared striding over the horizon toward us.

"*Oy vey,*" Kittelman said.

"You can say that again," the Tsaddik said.

"A mile high," I said.

"Give or take," the Tsaddik said.

"*Oy vey,*" Kittelman said.

"The trouble is," the Tsaddik said, "against gods the spells sometimes don't work."

"Mechanicals," I said. "Don't worry. Mechanicals will see us through."

"Mechanicals aren't so bad," the Tsaddik said.

The war god stood outlined against the blue sky. He looked at us. He spoke: "FEE FI FO FUM . . ."

Irving Kittelman said: "A fan of Let's Pretend?"

"It's probably the translator," I said. "In reality he's probably saying something entirely different."

"NONSENSE," Montu said, "I LEARNED THAT FROM A LITTLE HUMIE WITH A BRIEFCASE AND A BUSINESS SUIT."

"God-like hearing, too," the Tsaddik said.

"Something's fishy," I said. "Someone's been meddling in this galaxy—"

"HE SAID HUMIES TASTE GOOD!"

"We'd better go," the Tsaddik said.

"Let's go," Kittelman said.

"I think we'd better go," I agreed.

"BUT THAT *YOU* HUMIES WILL TASTE *ESPECIALLY* GOOD!"

"Us?" I said.

"*Nu?*" the Tsaddik said.

"Well?" Kittelman said.

"Damn jumper doesn't seem to work," I said.

"WELL," Montu said, stretching out a long giant arm, "TASTING'S BELIEVING."

"Make a spell," I yelled.

"Make a spell," Kittelman yelled.

"I'll make a spell," the Tsaddik said. "After all, what's to lose?" *Puff.*

The god was gone.

"Hey," Kittelman said, "that's really something. Vanished. Not a trace."

"Boy," I said, "I've really got to hand it to you. I'll say. You really made him take off, all right, Tsaddik, old pal; I don't mind telling you I was a bit worried there, boy-oh-boy. By the way, where did he go?"

"Hey, fellas," a tiny voice piped from somewhere.

"Huh?" Kittelman said.

"Come on, fellas," the tiny voice whined, "cut it out. What did you do?"

"Down by your toe," the Tsaddik said.

"Yawzeee!" Kittelman exclaimed.

"You fellas don't play fair," the tiny voice complained bitterly.

"Really a very minor spell," the Tsaddik said.

"You've made him small," I said wonderingly. "You've made Montu the war god small."

"I'll get you for this!" the tiny voice tweeted. A tiny fist shook at us.

"Uh-uh," the Tsaddik said.

"Uh-uh?" I said.

"Not small," the Tsaddik said.

"No, huh?" I said.

"Not?" Kittelman said.

"He stayed the same," the Tsaddik said.

"The same," I said.

"It's us," the Tsaddik said.

"I'll get even," the tiny voice piped miserably, "you wait and see."

"I've made us big," the Tsaddik said.

"B-B-B-Big?" Kittelman said.

"DON'T! DON'T DON'T!" the Tsaddik shrieked.

"Don't move! Don't breathe. One step and we've blotted out Egypt! We'd never hear the end of it!"

I used the jumper.

"Works again, huh?" the Tsaddik said.

We were in the gray-in-between.

"We back to normal?" I asked.

"It depends on what you mean by normal," the Tsaddik said. "If you mean size—our original size has been restored."

"That's nice," Irving Kittelman said. "So where are we now?"

"Taking a coffee break," I said. "We've earned one."

The Tsaddik went *puff*.

"Thanks," I said.

"It's Sanka," the Tsaddik said. "Won't keep you awake at night."

"Other things will," I said. We drank our coffee from steaming cups.

"Look," the Tsaddik said. "We've got to make a beginning. So far everyone we've found has been wrong."

"I've noticed," I said. "You've got an idea?"

"*Ahvadeh*, let's go pick up Moses."

"Sure. Just like that, huh?"

"Why not?"

"And *where* do we find him?" I asked.

The Tsaddik nodded. "Where else?" he said. "In front of Chock full o' Nuts."

The Lund Casebook: Five

We were moving along at a pretty good clip. You couldn't see much of the city down below because of the smoke. It looked to be a large spread but the smoke had blackened the streets and buildings. After a while we left the city behind; highways choked with traffic zigzagged below us. The air turned from black to gray.

"We're back in the gray-in-between, huh?" Wanda asked.

"Air pollution, sweetheart. The more advanced a society gets, the more air pollution it has; it's sort of a status symbol."

"Gee, Lund kid, you know everything, don't you?"

"Sure. That's what they keep me around for. This is probably the most advanced society ever."

The puller was zeroing in on a huge hundred-story building plunked down in the middle of a field. A tall wire fence enclosed the structure. The building, I saw, had no windows. We landed by the front door.

"We go in, just like that?" Wanda said. "No invitation or nothin'?"

"Why not? It'll take too long to drill a hole in the wall. We caseworkers, you know, can take care of ourselves."

The door opened automatically as we approached; we stepped in; it closed behind us.

The woman seated at the desk said, "Yes?"

The puller was still pulling. Our destination was somewhere inside and up. But behind the woman iron bars blocked our way. I saw at once there were two courses of action open to me. I could calmly explain the situation to this woman and allow reason, intelligence and humie intuition to do its stuff, or I could be more dramatically—but less reasonably—persuasive. Long years of caseworker experience have given me uncommon insight into the humie heart. I did the only thing possible.

The twelve-tailed, thirteen-headed Snizil the image projector produced sent the woman screaming down a side corridor. A button on her desk retracted the bars into the ceiling.

"Always look for buttons," I told Wanda as we went down a wide, gleaming hallway. "Without buttons these advanced societies aren't worth a damn."

We took an empty elevator up.

"Now," I said, "we switch from the puller, which is locked on this Myron creep, to the old finder and see what we find. Right, baby?"

"You've got my vote, Lund kid. I'm just along for the ride, remember?"

The "personal" beam began to sing ten soprano arias at once, hit a crescendo as we swung by the ninety-eighth floor and I reached for the stop button.

The "personal" beam pointed down another long corridor. We made tracks, turned a corner. More bars and three guys stood before us. The smallest of the three held up a hand.

"You have a pass, of course," he said.

"Of course they do," the tall man said. "Without a pass they couldn't have gotten up here."

"No one gets up here without a pass," the middle man said.

The bloated nine-tentacled Gliff from Nimble 12 that sprang from the image projector sent all three racing down the hall.

I found the button on the wall and the bars vanished into the ceiling.

We were facing a very wide white doorway.

"Lund kid," Wanda said, "we two been through a lot together and I haven't squawked yet (not much, anyway), but this is something I feel deeply; this is something I've got to tell you. It has to do with how princesses have more experience than most folks, more savvy, more pizzazz; more savoir-faire, in fact; 'cause they're princesses, see? So this thing I gotta tell you is simply this: DON'T OPEN THAT DOOR! Jinx, baby! The hex sign. Heap big trouble. Snake eyes, kid. . . ."

"Sorry," I said with some dignity. "We caseworkers never let terrible danger stand in our way. Besides, this is gonna be child's play."

I opened the door.

It was a very large white-walled room and it was crowded with people. All shapes and sizes, colors and costumes. It looked like open house at a humie fair. A babble of variegated tongues bounced off the four walls. Nobody paid much attention to us. It was a giant mill-in.

Wanda said: "We in the right place?"

"Uh-huh."

"It sure don't *look* like the right place."

"Looks are sometimes deceiving (I hope)."

"I mean this bunch doesn't seem grateful that you're gonna save it."

"This bunch is probably too confused to know any better."

"You think so?"

"Sure. How could they know I'm going to save 'em? I haven't told them yet."

"So tell 'em already."

"All in good time, sweetheart." I held up the translator. "First we double-check." I aimed at the crowd and listened:

"Behold, I go out from thee, and I will entreat the Lord that the swarms of flies may depart from Pharaoh, from his servants, and from his people, tomorrow: but let not Pharaoh deal deceitfully any more in not letting the people go to

sacrifice to the Lord. . . . Yes, that's it, all right . . . certainly the way to say it . . . and I will too . . . most assuredly . . . as soon as the Lord ceases this rather tiresome current miracle—no doubt it's another one of his endless tests . . . naturally . . . what else could it be?—and lets me get on with the job. . . . Still . . . maybe '*see here*' would be better than '*behold*' . . . ? Less forceful, of course, but more idiomatic . . . then again . . ."

"So I say, '*Shall I go and smite these Philistines?*' And He says, '*Arise, go down to Keilah; for I will deliver the Philistines into thine hand,*' so I do and look what happens! I land here. Lemme tell you something; that's the last time I ever listen to *Him*. . . ."

"Napoleon's war plans? Never! Death before I divulge my war plans!"

"Sure, I'm smart. Actually I've got quite a reputation back home. Back home it's always King Solomon this and King Solomon that: build a temple; raise a levy; go out and get married again: it's never anything easy—but *this?* I'll be darned if I can figure *this* out. . . ."

"Atomic energy, ha! It's the green eye-in-the-sky that does it all. I, Hans Kreegle, the world's greatest scientist, know that for a fact! Go on, quote me if you want to. I don't care. . . ."

"I'll say Shazam! and break outta this place. Any minute now I just say Shazam! . . . you watch and see if I don't. . . ."

"By my long black beard, a Jewish state in Palestine is an *absolute* necessity. . . ."

"Now let me make one thing perfectly clear: I *am* Richard Nixon and I *am* President of these United States. . . ."

I shrugged. "They seem diverse enough. And the translator registers multiple tongues. That's the give-away, kid; this is our bunch, all right."

"So it's all over, eh?"

"It sure looks that way."

"The leak's plugged."

"Well-ll, almost."

"There's more yet?"

"When isn't there?"

"I knew it, I just knew it!"

"Now, there's nothing to get steamed up over—"

"I bet it's gonna be something hard, too; it always is with you, Lund kid."

"Hard? What's so hard about rounding up a couple of history books?"

The girl stared at me. "That's what we gotta do? History books?"

"From the different time tracks. Sure. About three or four dozen books, actually. More or less. That should do it."

"Do what? You gonna *read* books?"

"Skim books. It's got to be done, sweetheart; how else can I figure out where these characters go?"

"You needn't bother," a familiar voice called out; it seemed to come from mid-air.

"Hm-m-m," I said. "That would be Myron, naturally. I've been expecting him."

Wanda said, "Now we're in for it, eh? There's going to be fighting and killing and hairpulling, huh?"

"Hardly," I said. "Where are you, Myron, you creep you. Come out and show yourself."

Across the room part of the wall drew back. A window appeared a few feet from the ceiling. Some of the crowd down below turned to gaze up at it; the rest ignored it.

"Allow me to introduce my friends," Myron said from behind the glass, his voice projecting into the room. "This is Dr. Bundy"—he indicated a small, round man with a pencil mustache standing by his side—"and this is Professor Lark." The prof was a long, skinny galoot with a pointed beak and burning eyes who hovered over Myron's left shoulder. Both were dressed in white. They didn't bother saying hello.

"Well, Myron old kick," I said, "the jig's up, you know."

"Indeed?"

"You can count on it, fella."

"I can?"

"Take my word for it, cousin: it's endsville."

Myron chuckled. "I wouldn't be so sure of that if I were you."

I waved a hand. "Come off it, brother. You real estate agents are all alike. You think you know it all just because you take down the big end of a touch. Well, there're other things in life besides dough—a whole lot of 'em. One time I made a list, see? And there must have been ten other things on that list if I recall rightly . . . things money couldn't buy. All kinds of things . . . that I don't happen to remember just right now. Yeah, you gung-ho money boys give me a pain. Where you tripped up, buddy, was letting me get a line on you. If you'd laid low I might never have run across you and your cache of leakies here. Got some kind of umbrella over 'em, don't you? Something that fouls up the finder? Yeah, you birds come equipped with all kinds of toys. But you had to go in for the grandstand play, had to turn up and try to buy me. Had to posture, strut and boast—"

"Hey, Lund kid, he didn't do all them things."

"I know," I told the girl. "But I got this speech memorized. It's the standard caseworker speech. Don't get to make it every day, you know." To Myron I said, "Now it's all over, guy, finished; these babies come back with me. I suppose I should thank you for rounding them up, for storing them all in one neat pile for me. But let's not kid ourselves, Myron old thing, I know you weren't doing me any favors. You made a booboo, Myron, that's all, and blew the game. Tough luck, fella."

"Booboo?" Myron said.

Professor Lark said: "Tsk, tsk. A sure sign."

Dr. Bundy said, "His voice, you know, it seems to be issuing . . . er . . . from that little black object. . . ."

Wanda said: "The opposition folds just like that? No fireworks, no nothin'?"

"Regulations," I pointed out, "inexorable laws of the galaxies. Oh sure, he'd like to have another lick at it, no doubt about that, honey; there's a lot of gravy bubbling around in this deal. But what can he do? His hands are tied. It's not just the Real Estate Commission, or the Global Tax Administration or the Intergalactic Investigating Subcommittee, although any one of those would be bad enough. It's the corps itself; no one wants to monkey with the corps anymore, not since they got that tie in with the Galactic Pension Fund; a being never knows in these hard, uncertain times when he'll have to draw on his pension; he wouldn't want it held up; not even someone as well fixed as our buddy here. Right, Myron?"

Myron sighed. "Who would dare flout the Pension Fund?"

"See, princess?" I said.

"No one is more law-abiding than I," Myron said.

"I guess so," Wanda said.

"When it comes to a law," Myron said, "I always *observe* it."

"I gotta hand it to you, Lund kid—" Wanda said.

"Laws and holidays," Myron said. "Especially holidays. But laws too."

"—you sure had this one figured right," Wanda said.

"Modesty prevents me from listing all the subtle stratagems that brought us to this point," I told her. "Maybe some other time."

"But I *am* Richard Nixon," a voice from the crowd said.

"Yes," Myron mused, "I have observed laws come and go,

but the power of money, it seems, remains constant (subject, of course, to natural economic fluctuations—but then, what isn't?). And that is why, in fact, I have brought you here."

"Brought me here?" I said.

"Law and order," Myron said.

"Me? Here?" I said. "Ha. Ha."

"To observe how it functions here in this very advanced society. Here in 1986 on a cloudy June day. And to have you participate, of course, for surely to know the law one must *experience* it."

"Hold it, bright boy," I sneered. "Just consider awhile: he who messes with me takes on the corps! Etc. and so forth. Especially and *so forth* . . . if you get me."

"Perish the thought. *Me* mess with *you?* How unseemly. However, dear boy, if you chose to follow me to these far-out co-ords—of your own free will—and just *happened* to run afoul of the local laws . . ."

"Ha! You wouldn't dare!"

"Me, no. Them, yes."

"Them?"

"The indigens."

"Lark," Bundy said.

"And Bundy," Lark said.

"You *know* how indigens are," Myron said. "They have this *thing* about their quaint autochthonous laws."

"Thing?" Wanda said.

"Why yes. They like to see them enforced."

"It's an indigen's privilege," Lark said.

"It's an indigen's *right,*" Bundy said.

"I see you two guys been well schooled," I said.

"And naturally, who can hold *me* responsible for what *they* do?" Myron said. "Bylaw 809X2, you know."

"I told him. I said: don't open that door. Watch out for that ugly white door," Wanda said.

"Bah! What can they do?"

"Nothing," Bundy said, "if you have your mental certificates."

"This is the place," Lark said, "where we put those without mental certificates."

"Or with expired mental certificates," Bundy said.

"Or invalid mental certificates," Lark said.

"Oh dear me, yes," Myron said, "they do have a going concern here."

"Here being the booby-hatch," Lark said.

"Where you're at, in fact," Myron said. "None of these folks here—as you might have gathered—have their mental certificates. And some of them even belong here. Crazy, you know. Oh, it's quite legal, I assure you."

"The very letter of the law," Lark said.

"Quite right," Bundy agreed. "But naturally, you clever people *have* your mental certificates. Hm-m-m?"

"Surely," Lark said, "they didn't venture out *without* their mental certificates, did they?"

"Are you guys kidding?" I said.

"Oh dear," Myron said. "Too bad."

"So what about it, buster?" I demanded.

"Maybe we should run for it?" Wanda whispered, "while we got the chance."

"Forget it," I said. "We get on with the job. You don't really figure these two-bit natives are gonna go up against an invulnerable caseworker, do you?"

"Us no," long and short said. "Him yes. Our deputy."

"Authorized deputy," Myron beamed, "and as legal as pie. I may not be as well stocked, gizmo-wise, as the average caseworker, but the home office does thoughtfully provide us with a few diverting gadgets."

"Oh yeah?" I growled, making a grab for my traveling bag,

ready to unload a sample of caseworker woe (if I could find one in time), when something went:

Pzzzzzuzl.

And all the lights all over the joint went "blap."

Courtney: Eight

"He's always here, right on the corner," Irving Kittelman said, "honest."

"No one doubts your word," I said.

"Since when?"

"Well, by golly, the Lund report bears you out."

"Lund report?"

"Before your arrival."

"Ah, before I joined the team."

"Yeah, I suppose you might say that."

I repressed a shudder. The Tsaddik, meanwhile, was giving the old environment the bright eye. "Greenberg," he said, "always liked it here. The excitement. Especially when they were rioting over there at that school. He said it reminded him of the little country."

Kittelman said, "You mean the old country."

The Tsaddik shook his head. "Little country. Remember who you're dealing with."

I sighed. "That was before his time too."

"I got a lot to learn, eh?" Kittelman said.

I shrugged. "If we don't do something quick to plug this stupid leak, don't worry, you won't have to bother. No one will."

I got the reader out and ran it over the street. One hundred sixteenth Street. Columbia University. Chock full o' Nuts. Garbage disposal. Subway. The scene was just how poor old Lund had described it. Humie and vehicular traffic still swamped the territory. Air pollution peppered the atmosphere. An orange sun shone through the haze. But no sign of this Moses lad. Lund hadn't mentioned garbage disposal. Maybe Moses got tangled up in that? It didn't seem too likely, though. Garbage disposal seemed to be only a box. Boy, talk about being primitive. So much for the old reader.

Next I got the finder out and gave it a whirl. Set for "personal," if there'd been any leak material in this co-ord it would have sounded off on the double. Not a squeak. Yeah, well, there you are.

"Maybe we should ask someone?" the Tsaddik said.

"Sure. Everybody knows that crazy guy," Kittelman said. "Just ask anyone. Go on. You'll see. Just any one at all."

The three of us marched into Chock full o' Nuts. Business was slow.

"There's a guy," I said to one of the girls behind the counter, "who stands in front of your store?"

"So?" she said.

"With the sign," Kittelman said.

"And the beard," the Tsaddik said. "Moses would have a beard, of course."

"Right," Kittelman said.

"Moses?" the waitress said.

"We want him," I said.

The girl shook her head. "Who?"

"You new here?" Kittelman said.

"Me?" she said. "Cut it out."

"Maybe you've just been too busy to notice," Kittelman said. "This guy with the sign is well known."

"Guy? Sign? You think I'm blind or something? There's never been no guy with no sign near this place, take it from a waitress who knows. I mind my own business, right? But I got eyes, right? So ask, ask anyonc clsc. Go on. Ask. Ask."

"You won't mind?" the Tsaddik asked.

"It's not an insult," I pointed out.

"We gotta know," Kittelman said.

"So go know," she said.

We went.

Five minutes later we were back on the street out on the corner. The waitress stuck her head through the door: "See?" she said.

"Yeah, sure, honey," Kittelman said.

"Boy," I said.

"They're all *crazy* in there," Kittelman whispered. "Too much work has rotted their minds. . . . I've always maintained that physical labor was bad for people. Look, I live just a couple blocks away; you think I could be wrong on something like this? Why, that guy's a blasted landmark."

"Dirty work," I said, "could account for it."

"None of these advanced places are too clean," the Tsaddik said. "*Shmutsik*. You think, maybe, Moses became disgusted and went away."

"He was never here," I said. "Not really. Which is to say not anymore. These leakies, you know, take them out of a spot they don't belong in and they leave practically no trace."

The Tsaddik lifted an eyebrow. "Take them out?"

"I see you've caught the catch-phrase," I said. "This will take a bit of doing, but it's just barely possible we can run down the sequence. Maybe."

I pressed a button and we jumped into the gray-in-between.

"The trouble is," I said, "that this stupid jumper makes matters worse. Boy, what we really need is the old dissolver. Then we could sort of flit back along the possibilities and peek out every now and then. The old dissolver, of course, is what we ain't got. But does that daunt us? You bet it does!"

Everything was a smoky gray now. We were right in between the co-ords. But by working close to the boundaries we could look through. What we saw was Chock full o' Nuts. The corner. The street. The university. The same scene. But different each time. Like flipping pages in a book.

Each one a slightly different possibility. This stuff can get pretty tedious after a while. And if we kept it up long enough Chock full o' Nuts would probably blink out and a cavern or dugout or something would take its place. That would be a different track. And that, of course, is what we didn't want.

The jumper, meanwhile, was riding a stop-and-go roller coaster.

Pop.

Pop.

Pop.

Bad for humies with loose teeth, tight stomachs and a general nervous condition. Me, naturally. And anyone else who came along for the trip. And stayed till the end.

The end came in no time at all. Or a lot of time, depending on how you looked at it. But then, most things do, don't they?

"Enough already," the Tsaddik wheezed.

"Hey!" Kittelman called. "Hey! Hey!"

We'd been moving pretty fast. I hit the button.

I pulled short, reversed directions and hopped back a couple of frames.

The guy with the beard was at his post all right. And he looked kind of sour. But who could blame him?

"Well, it only took fifty jumps," I sighed, trying to stop shaking. "One frame out of fifty." I snapped my fingers. "We could have missed it like that."

"Yeah, that's him," Kittelman said. "The crazy guy. The nut."

"Moses," the Tsaddik said. "But he doesn't look happy. What kind of job is that for Moses?"

"When they leak," I said, "they sometimes become disoriented."

I worked the jumper controls to achieve duration, hooked the finder onto our quarry, speeded up the whole sequence and watched and followed him through two long weeks of snappy activities. It took all of a few eye-blinks. A rooming house; the street corner; long trudging walks in a park. This Moses was in a rut.

"Very bad disorientation," I explained.

"How does he live?" the Tsaddik asked.

"Poorly," Kittelman said. "You can see that."

I said, "State aid, no doubt. These leak cases have their compensations. Survival knowledge leaks through, too. And rudimentary indigen mother tongues. Knowledge on how to fill out welfare forms. Which charities to go to. The best place to buy used clothes—"

After a while Moses started to fade out. In an instant he was gone.

"What's happening?" Kittelman demanded. "We lost him?"

"The pay-off," I said. "Someone's using a puller out there, that's what. Very sophisticated device. Very clever. Only we're hooked on. How about that?"

We popped out of the gray ether.

We were in a large, white-walled, very crowded room. Humies of all descriptions were pacing back and forth, mumbling and murmuring to themselves and others. It was totally chaotic. There were no windows.

"It's like a mad house," Kittelman moaned.

"Quite right," a voice said.

"Look out!" another voice called. "He's got a—"

"Lund!" I shrieked. "We thought you were canceled—"

Something went:

Kazzzzzoogl.

And all the lights, lamps, candles and fireflies everywhere, all at once, seemed to short out.

The Tsaddik Himself: Six

Who could sleep with all this noise, this constant talking? I sat up—I was lying on the floor, it seems—and opened my eyes.

The man called Lund was saying, "—stripped clean . . . I woke up and the traveling bag was gone; it would be of course . . . no way to communicate with the higher-ups. No way at all. It's curtains, all right. . . ."

Curtains? There weren't even any windows in the place.

Courtney was saying, "We walked right into it, by golly . . . there's a word for that. . . ."

"Sap," Lund said. "That's the word."

"Yeah," Courtney said, "that's it all right; it sure gives a caseworker satisfaction to come up with the right word—but not as much as you might think."

"Are we doomed?" the girl Wanda asked. "Is that it? Are we all doomed? I don't *feel* doomed; no headache, no nasal drip, no nothing. . . ."

"Look—" Irving Kittelman was saying. "All I was doing—right?—was minding my own business. I wasn't bothering anyone, was I? I can get witnesses. There must be some kind of law covering that. An innocent bystander's law . . . the uninvolved . . . the onlooker . . . the non-participant. . . . What we oughtta do right away is present my case to the highest authorities . . . get a hearing set up; we could petition, maybe. . . ."

I looked around at the rest of the crowd. There weren't two people dressed alike and no one was paying attention to anyone else. Yet everyone was talking. The obvious mark of a prestigious gathering. No doubt these were all great personages, but who could recognize anyone? No one looked very happy; actually, they all looked *oysgemutshet*. Well, they'd been through a lot, of course.

I turned back to my friends and said hello.

Courtney looked up.

"Huh?" he said.

He sat bolt upright and grabbed Lund by the arm.

Lund raised an eyebrow. "Yes-s-s?"

"He said hello," Courtney hissed.

"Yeah," Lund said. "So what?"

"We understood him."

"He has a speech defect?"

"OUR TRANSLATORS ARE GONE!"

Lund's mouth fell open.

Irving Kittelman said, "I demand a lawyer!"

"We can understand him, too," Courtney yelled. "All along we've been able to understand him!"

Lund turned to Wanda. "Say something."

"You *sure* we're doomed, Lund kid?"

"Don't count on it, sweetheart." To Courtney he said, "What gives here?"

"He's a wonder-worker."

Lund said, "Yeah, so it seems. Is this his main bit, or does he have a second act, too?"

"It's the speech spell," I explained. "The one I used before; it's still activated. To tell the truth, I forgot to turn it off."

"You still have your spells?" Courtney said.

"Why shouldn't I?"

Lund said, "His *spells?*"

"They didn't take your spells away, Tsaddik, old buddy?"

"They?" Lund said. "There's only this Myron creep. Some salesman from Universe End. What they?"

"The real estate outfit?" Courtney groaned. "They're responsible? They're the ones?"

"One. Not ones. Better leave off the *s*. There's no *s* in one."

"Boy, what a disgrace," Courtney said. "What if someone should find out?"

"Don't worry," Lund said. "After we're canceled, it won't matter."

"Canceled?"

"Do they know I'm an American citizen?" Irving Kittelman demanded. "Is there no American Consul around here?"

"Who could take spells from me?" I said. "Spells, after all, aren't mechanicals. A Tsaddik and his spells, you realize, aren't soon parted."

"I hadn't realized," Courtney said.

"In fact, they're never parted," I said.

"What can he do?" Lund asked.

"He can do anything!" Courtney said.

"Anything?" Lund said.

"*You* name it," Courtney said. "*He* can do it."

Lund nodded: "Cosmic dribble."

"Sure," Courtney said. "Precisely."

"It figures," Lund said.

"Any Tsaddik would do as much," I pointed out. "Your Myron, by the way; I think I met him. In Egypt. And in that other place. Which, come to think of it, is probably this place."

"How would you know?" Kittelman asked.

"Particle to air ratio."

"Wait a minute," Lund said. "Myron knows about your . . . er, abilities?"

"Why shouldn't he? Actually, there was a job he wanted me to do. Blow up some place. I said no."

"Oh-oh," Courtney said.

"Yeah," Lund said. "If Myron knows, how come the Tsaddik's still here?"

"Where else should I be?"

"Anywhere. But not here."

"Can't be done," I said.

"He's right!" Courtney said. "I'm caught in his food spell!"

"You're *what?*"

"We're inseparable," Courtney said.

"Anyway," I said, "Myron probably didn't recognize me. I had a beard then, you know. But it's gone away since."

"That's right," Myron said. "I didn't recognize him. Gracious, I *really* must be slipping."

Then there was nothing.

The vast emptiness engulfed us. Courtney, Lund, the girl, Kittelman. And myself. The others were gone. The building was gone. This wasn't the gray-in-between. This place was nothing. But I'd been here, too. A natural consequence of wide travels. The last time I'd seen Myron I had passed through this very spot (on the way to third person).

I recalled the disturbing effect of that time. I made a light. I made a platform for standing. A reassuring word seemed in order; I produced one. "It's all right," I said, "we're nowhere."

"I guessed as much," Wanda said. "No kidding; it just came to me."

"Is this better or worse than the other mess?" Kittelman demanded.

"It looks worse, but logic says it can't be," Courtney said. "Can it?"

"I'm going to be seasick," Lund told me.

I made the calm stomach spell.

"Incredible," Lund said. "Has anyone tried to merchandise this?"

"Cosmic dribble," Courtney reminded him.

"But there's a fortune here."

I said, "What's happened is that this Myron person has put us out in nowhere. Under the delusion that I can't find my way back. Last time this happened Greenberg was here; between us we got lost. *Nu*, these things happen. Broad conclusions, however, should not be drawn."

"We go back!" Lund said.

"Tsaddik, old pal, can you dig up our traveling bags?" Courtney asked.

"When we're back," I said.

"Why don't we go someplace *nice* instead?" Kittelman said.

I made the back spell.

"Dear me," Myron said, "you are persistent, aren't you?"

I made the traveling bag spell.

I made the protective bubble spell. Just in time.

"Here come the devils," I said.

The bubble was engulfed in flame.

"Devil attacks," I said, "can be very nasty."

The bubble started to melt.

Myron seemed to hover above us. A herd of shrieking witches, goblins and devils poured out of a hole in the ceiling, flayed at our bubble, unleashed streams of fire, pitch, tar, lava and what seemed to be a new brand of instant dissolving ointment. They certainly warmed up to their work, these folks—eyes wide, gleaming mouths stretched into awesome grins. Pointy teeth. Red tails. To tell the truth—despite certain philosophical differences, unbridgeable naturally—I had to admire their enthusiasm. They put their hearts into a job. Of course, when it came to soul, it was something else.

"The bubble's melting!" Kittelman screamed.

I made the reinforcement spell.

The reinforcement started to melt.

"One Tsaddik," I said, "has his hands full when it comes to a bunch of devils."

I made a river flood through the hole in the ceiling. The river turned to acid. "See?" I said.

"Say, what's this Myron trying to do?" Courtney yelled.

"Cancel us, I should think," Lund said.

"Boy, that's not cricket at all. They could have his license for that."

"*They* would probably never know."

"We ought to send a complaint off pronto, that's what. Now that we got our senders back—"

"Well-ll, this is indigen's work. These devils *are* indigens, after all," Lund shrugged. "We could go away, you know. You've got your jumper back; I've got my dissolver. Maybe that's what he wants."

"I'd rather roast!"

"That's coming, too," Wanda said.

"Any second now," Kittelman said.

"Anyway," Lund said, "it takes months to get a complaint processed."

"Wait a minute," I said. I looked out at the rest of the crowd. They were off to one side in the large white room. Our historical guests watching, but safe. On their side of the room nothing was happening. Certainly many of them were Tsaddikim. But did I dare bring them into the *tumel?* It seemed a big risk. What if someone was hurt? History would never be the same. Already it began to look as if history was a thing of the past. I thought it over.

Muddle was too empty to bother with; everyone would be out sightseeing. No help from Muddle. But surely a Tsaddik or two could be found somewhere else close by? A man as well traveled as myself should have no trouble finding a Tsaddik or two. Right?

The swarming Hasidim who finally dived on the devils through the hole in the ceiling were dressed in long black fluttering garments and wide-brimmed hats. Their beards bristled and their eyes were fierce. Naturally they were upset.

The knowledge spell had told them what was happening.

The truth spell had convinced them it was all true.

The transportation spell had brought them—*hendim-pendim*—from New Jersey to New York. A veritable treasure trove of Tsaddikim. And I'd almost forgotten about them.

"It's a drove of Hasidim," I said to my friends. "This will make things better."

"How much better?" Kittelman asked.

"Will it make things *good?*" Wanda asked.

"Good," I said, "is probably a long way off."

Courtney said: "Myron is still watching."

He rode above the action, I saw. "I could make an anti-hover spell," I suggested. "Or I could send him off to the frozen wastes or the burning desert or the place of constant, unalleviated darkness. I could also give him a tummy ache; he wouldn't like that."

"It wouldn't bother him much," Courtney said. "Sad but true. He's an extra-terrestrial, you know. If he were prone to all these spells, to all the adversities of leak activity, he'd be no good for the job, would he?"

"But you were caught in my food spell," I pointed out.

"Let's not mention that too often," Courtney said. "The thing is, Tsaddik, it's all a matter of tools, of implements, of mechanicals. Private enterprise has supplied Myron with some pretty nifty mechanicals."

"The best," Lund said.

"Ours are pretty good too, of course," said Courtney.

"But his are better," Lund said.

"We got more," Courtney said. "We can stop reality."

"Yeah," Lund said, "for five whole minutes, whatever that's worth. What we need here is a diversion."

"This isn't diverting enough?" Wanda asked.

"Confusion," Lund said. "Under cover of confusion we could spirit off our leakies, sort them out, catalogue them. . . ."

They were all looking at me.

"Well, yes," I said, "there's nothing hard about creating *confusion*. It takes a minimum of talent. We'd want to choose the right one, though."

"Any one at all," Lund said.

"Let's not be fussy," Courtney said.

"Metaphysical confusion?" I asked.

"Wrong kind," Lund said.

"Spiritual?"

"Too tame. Look—it's got to be devastating. Something awful, something *physical*."

"Oh!" I said. "Physical can be very potent. I see what you mean. Well, near Muddle, my shtetl, we may have just the thing. A whole army. A real *krank*. And they're very physical."

"An army?" Courtney said.

"I'll show you," I said.

"Good grief!" Wanda gasped. "King Casy!"

King Casimir the Fourth was mounted on his fiery steed. He charged through a hole in the wall, sword outthrust, brows knit, eyes glowering.

Desperately he reined in his horse, glanced behind him.

"See?" I said.

In a moment the rest of the army appeared. Bouncing, rolling, pushing, sliding, tripping, crawling through the hole. I made the expansion spell for more room. Short soldiers and tall, fat and skinny, wide and narrow. In an instant there was more confusion than anyone could want.

Hasidim, king's men and devils boiled and bubbled along the floor, up and over the walls. Black, oily smoke rose to the ceiling. Flames sputtered and died. The whole building seemed to shake with locked bodies, clashing swords and screaming mouths.

"Very confusing," Lund admitted.

"A veritable beehive," Courtney said.

"But is it safe?" Kittelman asked.

That reminded me. I made a protective shell around our remnants from history. They were standing transfixed on their side of the room. They'd even stopped talking. This scene, no doubt, was going to add whole volumes to theology. If our guests got back to where they belonged, that is.

Myron, meanwhile, was nowhere in sight.

"Some *plonternish*, eh?" I said, not without pride.

"It's a knockout, sweetie," Wanda said.

Sweetie?

"Now it's our turn," Lund said. "Quick, while we've got the chance, we steal these leakie guys—preferably to some nice quiet, impenetrable place—and start sorting them out."

"Yeah, that's what we do," Courtney said, "quick, while we've got the chance. That's it, all right. . . ."

A round, shimmering circle was beginning to glow in the center of the turmoil. The turmoil made room for it, edged away toward the four corners and the walls. The circle was opaque, blue in color, and it kept growing.

Courtney turned to Lund. "Do you see what I see?"

"I see it," Lund said, "but I don't believe it."

"It's impossible," Courtney said.

"We in trouble again?" Irving Kittelman asked miserably, peering from behind his round spectacles.

"We were never out," Wanda said.

"Should I make a spell?" I asked.

"It's too late for spells," Courtney said.

"This is the end," Lund said flatly.

Courtney clutched his head: "Why?" he asked. "Why did this have to happen now? Why?"

Courtney: Nine

"This is a fine kettle of fish," Assistant Case Supervisor Shmelk said sourly. He was backing out of the transport oval. "Easy does it there." A large contraption was being unloaded. Boy, they hadn't even bothered to send a humie work crew along. Two furry-toed Nicks wrestled with the machine that looked like a long, golden telescope on tripods. A sleek-bodied Temp was trying to help out, but his tentacles kept getting in the way. Well, at least that part was still SOP.

Lund whispered in my ear: "We'll bluff it."

"Are you kidding?" I said.

"Isn't there something in the Union laws about this?" he demanded.

"For this to happen," I said, "they probably busted the Union."

Shmelk spotted us.

"Ah!" he said simply. It was enough.

"Look, Mr. Shmelk—" I began.

"A black day," Shmelk said, "that's what it is. When supervisory personnel have to go into the field. By grechens, this will cause a rumpus."

"Actually," I said, "there's one going on right now. As a matter of fact, it's almost the end of the world here; only don't worry, we've got things in hand—"

"There's no doubt about that," Lund said. "Under control. A-one. Ship-shape. We were just gonna wrap this one up, chief. Any second now."

"You bet!" I said.

"Quiet," Shmelk said. "Lund. You were supposed to be canceled."

"I can explain that."

"Courtney. We've been getting your reports."

"Well, sure," I said. "I'm very prompt in getting my reports out. It's the mark of the well-trained caseworker to speedily prepare—"

"They were dreadful! A disgrace! Floor Supervisor Gazoom Velk was *very* upset. Imagine! Two caseworkers on one world—two supposedly experienced caseworkers—and everything going to the dogs." Shmelk looked around quickly. "Forget that last one, lads; don't want to get any dogs down on me. Live and let live, you know."

"Look, chief," Lund said. "We've got all the leakies rounded up. In one spot. All set to be sent back. How's that for service? You can't knock that, chief; all in one bunch—"

"Leakies? Where are they?"

"Over there, Mr. Shmelk," I said. "That gang on the far side of the room; the ones lying on the floor and fainting. Boy, it's finally gotten to 'em, hasn't it?"

"Leak shock," Lund said. "Sooner or later it gets them all."

"Caseworkers, too, it looks like," I said.

"Who are all these others?" Shmelk wanted to know.

"Others? Oh—those are devils, soldiers and Hasidim, boss. There's kind of a small war going on here. You see, boss, there's this real estate guy—"

"I know. I know," Shmelk said.

"You do?" Lund said.

"How can he know?" I asked.

"What are we encased in?" Shmelk demanded. "I presume that's the situation. Since we aren't being hit, pummeled and stepped on. And *they* are."

"So they are," Lund agreed.

"Yes, that's what's happening, all right," I said. "Meet the Tsaddik, boss; he's been kind of . . . er . . . helping out."

The Tsaddik said hello.

"It's a spell," I said. "The Tsaddik makes spells. We're encased in a protective bubble. Very useful, actually."

"A reinforced, protective bubble," the Tsaddik added.

"Spells?" Shmelk said. "Good gracious, what next? Look, lads, is there any way out of this bubble?"

I said, "We could make a hole, I guess. Right, Tsaddik?"

The Tsaddik nodded.

"Only we've got to be careful," I said. "It's pretty hectic out there."

"It's *dangerous* out there," Irving Kittelman said.

"Make a small hole," Shmelk said.

A small hole appeared. Screams, yells, groans, burst through it. A riot of shouts and curses. There were sounds of punching, slapping and stomping. All kinds of hitting noises.

"Boy, it really *isn't* safe," I said.

"Can we tone that down?" Shmelk said.

The Tsaddik made a volume-control spell.

Shmelk stuck his head through the hole:

"You there!" he called. "The humie from Universe End. Where are you?"

"It's no use, boss," I explained.

"He won't listen, chief," Lund said.

"Some beings," I said, "have no respect for authority."

"Yes-s-s?" a voice called back. It came from under a mound of squirming bodies.

Shmelk waved a paper.

"I've got a restraining order here," he shouted, "from the Real Estate Commission. You're to cease and desist at once, you hear? At once!"

"Someone snitched, eh?" Myron asked. Slowly he extracted himself from the mound of bodies. "Well, it's all been legal, you know; the letter of the law. No one's got a thing on me."

He stepped over to look at Shmelk's document. "Hm-m-m," he said. "This would have to happen. And just when I was about to land a big one. Oh, well . . . so many loose ends to watch. Two caseworkers on one world, no less. What an awful headache . . . not to mention this Tsaddik person . . ." Myron cast a baleful glance, fixed his tie, brushed off his suit, straightened his hat, clutched his briefcase and promptly dissolved. No more Myron.

A hand tapped on our bubble. A body lifted itself off the floor. "Look here," a mournful voice called, "there must be some fearful error. I am Bulbus the Monk. I *know* I don't belong here. . . ."

"That goes for me too, fellas," a tiny voice piped near the monk's elbow. "I didn't mean all that stuff about getting even. Honest. I'm all set to let well enough alone, if you'll just send me back—"

"Montu the war god!" I exclaimed.

"Caught in a spell, no doubt," the Tsaddik mused.

"Surely we don't need all this commotion now, lads?" Shmelk said.

"I suppose not," Lund said.

"We can dispense with it," I said. "And then some." I nodded at the Tsaddik.

Hasidim, soldiers, devils, disappeared. The protective bubble fell away. The holes in wall and ceiling sealed. The building was restored to its former self. Except for the horde of leakies that still remained. The blue opaque transport oval. The telescope thing. Shmelk. The work crew. The rest of us.

The work crew departed through the oval.

Shmelk sighed. "That's how to handle a job," he said.

"No doubt," I said. "When it's in its last stages."

"Yeah. When the ground work's already been laid," Lund said.

"At least it's quiet again," Wanda said.

"Chief," Lund said. "About that desist order—"

"Yeah, that's right—" I began.

A figure was stepping through the oval. "Let's get this over with," a scratchy voice grumbled.

"Doc Scrudge!"

The little humie looked at me. "You boys can't do anything right, can you?"

"Hey," Lund said. "Since when are office workers licensed for the field?"

"Special permit," Shmelk said. "Emergency heading. It'll look just *grand* on your case records, lads."

"Oh well," I said. "Making Corps Hero isn't everything. Who needs a five-rating jump, anyway?"

"Yeah," said Lund. "There are quiet satisfactions in life, too. They count for something."

"Like sleeping," I said. "Sleeping a lot can be very satisfying."

"Step aside," Doc Scrudge said. "We haven't got all day."

He began fingering knobs and buttons on the long machine. It started to hum, then vibrate.

"What is that thing?" I asked.

"It's a raiser, sport."

"A raiser?"

"We're raising Atlantis," Assistant Case Supervisor Shmelk said. "Seems there's an underwater continent out there called Atlantis, and we're raising her."

"Good grief, why?"

"Petitioned," Shmelk said. "A delegation petitioned the Galactic Council. Got wind of their imminent cancellation, somehow, and went over our heads. Highly irregular. So now we've got to raise this Atlantis for them to live on."

"Delegation?"

Shmelk produced a crumpled form: "The Wenzel people, the stone people, the frog people, the hulk people, the women people, the devil people—"

"Devil people?" Lund said.

"Devils are people, too," Shmelk said. "Under galactic law."

"But how did they get to you?" I exclaimed. "It's impossible. None of these beings use transporters . . . know about blast-offs . . . understand co-ords. Why, this world doesn't even know there's a Cosmos Corps!"

"—and the little people," Shmelk added.

"Of course," the Tsaddik yelled, "the little people are all travel agents!"

"Little people?" I said.

"My friend Greenberg. The homunculus."

"Oh yeah," I said. "I'd forgotten."

Doc Scrudge sighed. "It's done," he said.

"You've raised Atlantis?" I asked.

"The raiser's raised Atlantis, sport. I just push the buttons. Okay to go now?"

Shmelk said it was. Doc Scrudge weaved his way back through the oval and was gone.

"That was quick," I said.

"We'd better finish off here," Shmelk said nervously. "This leak's been in operation a long time."

"No problem there," Lund said. "We just have this guy here help us sort—"

"You have who what?" Shmelk said.

"Him there . . . er . . ."

"Where's Kittelman?" I asked.

Wanda looked at the Tsaddik. The Tsaddik looked at Lund. Lund looked at me.

"Don't look at me," I said. "What would I want with him?" We all looked around.

"Where the hell is he?" Lund demanded.

"Tsaddik?" I said.

The Tsaddik made a spell.

"So?" I said.

"Well—" the Tsaddik said.

"What is this?" Shmelk asked.

"He must be out of reach," the Tsaddik said. "It happens sometimes. But not often."

"This is fantastic," Lund said. "How could he just vanish?"

"He's important?" Shmelk asked.

"Without him," I said, "we're gonna have trouble getting the leakies home."

"Unless, of course, we've got time to dig up some history books," Lund said. "A couple encyclopedias, maybe, an almanac—"

"Good gracious," Shmelk shouted, "don't you realize we're almost out of time?"

"Yeah, it had occurred to me," Lund said.

"Say, Lund," I said.

"Huh?"

"Your dissolver—"

"What about it?"

"I just thought of something."

"Yeah?"

"You got your dissolver, of course?"

"My dissolver? Sure, I got my—Hey!"

"Oh boy," I said.

"Let me guess," Shmelk said.

"THAT CRAZY KID," Lund screamed, "HAS STOLEN MY DISSOLVER!"

"Restricted corps property in the hands of a native," Shmelk sighed. "Well, that does it! We'll never escape a hearing now."

"That ain't all we won't escape," Lund said.

"I'd better get back to the home office, lads," Shmelk said, springing for the oval. "There's no telling what pressing business has turned up in my absence. We assistant case supervisors, you know, are always on call-l-l. . . ."

"Doggone it," I said.

"Look at that," Lund said.

"Still pretty fast on his feet, all right."

"What we ought to do," Lund whispered, "is follow his example and get outta here, fast."

"What! And let this world blow up?"

Lund sighed. "We can't do that," he said. "We'd never live it down."

"Hold on," I said. "Just wait a second. Do you know how I got hold of this Kittelman in the first place?"

"How should I know that?" Lund demanded. "Do I look like a mind reader?"

"With the puller," I said.

"*Puller?*"

"Yeah! He's still gotta be hooked on!"

"Go!" Lund shouted. "Don't stand there wasting words. Go! Just go!"

I grabbed the jumper.

I went.

"No," Irving Kittelman said. "I'm not going back. It's nice here. I like it here. It's definitely very comforting here. Comfort has been something lacking in my life . . . a true absence at times . . . a desideratum, in fact. It doesn't seem fair to give it up now. I've observed, you know, that most things in life are unfair—I've spied that while trundling along; it's caught my attention—but to leave here, at this time, that would be *more* unfair than most. Maybe some other time; yes, I'll think it over."

"Look," I said, "it's all in your mind."

"I've considered that. So what? There are worse things in life; I'm prepared to put up with it. Offhand there are thousands of worse things . . . I could enumerate a couple, if you want . . ."

"You miss the point," I said.

"Oh? Which one is that?"

"You don't really get it," I said, "do you?"

"It's probably of small import."

"I'll speak plainly."

"Please do."

"YOU'RE STUCK IN YOUR MIND!"

"Who isn't?"

"Listen—you're *literally* stuck in your mind. What a crazy stunt! Don't you know what happens to natives who swipe corps property? *This* is what happens. Boy, what an awful place, just look at it: everything's spooky; those elongated bodies, those swarming colors, those bloated faces—"

"Actually, that's from a comic book called Plastic Man. Very popular a few decades ago . . ."

"Come on, Kittelman, this is no place for you. Believe me. Anything is better than this. This is unreal."

"My mind, unreal?"

"The whole human race is counting on you, Kittelman. Don't let them down. You'll never forgive yourself if you louse up the human race. Boy, there'll be nothing left. Imagine trying to explain that! Think of all the paper work involved. Have a heart, Kittelman, come back."

"Waddya mean, my mind's unreal?"

"Well, sure. It's all subjective, isn't it? Hold on, let me check it for you. I'll compute it for you. Anything for a pal, right? Circa 1943—that's where you are, Kittelman. Now you know, right? By golly, you were just a kid then. You see? That explains all these weird shapes—"

"I take it you can't make me return?"

"Make you? How can I make you go from your own mind? From any other place, sure; I just use the puller. From your mind, no."

"Then I'm not going."

"Don't make me beg, Kittelman; it's not dignified."

"It's *nice* here. See that voice?"

"*See* a voice?"

"Sure. That's Raymond from Inner Sanctum. Unforgettable. Where else can you see a voice except in a person's mind?"

"How about a nut house?"

"Look. You see the snow? When I was a kid, there used to be much more snow, everywhere; tons of it. Mountains. And block-long food markets with wooden stands. There used to be elevated trains all over the place—"

"So what?"

"It was nice."

"You just think so. Listen, it was like everything else. Temporary. If you don't get rid of that stuff, you've got a terrible pile up. It's got to go."

"Alan Ladd and Veronica Lake—remember—*The Glass Key*? Raymond Chandler's *The High Window*. The Falcon was on the radio. Duz did everything. Captain Marvel put out a giant two-hundred-page comic. But the Marvel Bunny never made the Marvel Family. Left out. It used to kill me, you know. I couldn't get over it. It seemed like *injustice*. They were singing 'Coming in on a Wing and a Prayer.' You had to have ration stamps. You bought war bonds. Everyone worked in war plants—"

"Say, that really sounds swell," I said. "War plants. Yeah, that's what we need some more of—war plants."

"You don't understand. In those days it was good."

"It just *seemed* good because you were a little kid."

"Oh, I don't know about that. Being a little kid wasn't all that hot. It had a lot of disadvantages. It had my mother. That was an awful disadvantage all by itself."

"Your mother?"

"Sure, I—oh-oh."

A gigantic female figure had begun to rise out of the mind-swarm, had begun to *grow*.

"That's her!" Kittelman shrieked.

"Your mother, huh?"

"We gotta hide!"

"It's your mind, fella."

"Quick! I'll think of something else. I'll make it go away. Tom Mix. Abie's Irish Rose. I Love a Mystery. The Black Hawks. Fred Allen. Looney Tunes and Merry Melodies. Good grief! It's still growing. It's growing, I tell you! Walter Winchell! Ginny Simms! Gene Autry! A Superman DC Publication! Kate Smith! MY GOD! THERE'LL BE NO ROOM FOR ANYONE ELSE!"

"That seems to be the idea," I said.

Everything else was being pushed aside now by the ballooning mother creature, was being squeezed and crushed.

"Run! Run!" Kittelman shrieked.

Giant eyes stared. Monstrous lips parted. A ringing, deafening voice articulated:

"DON'T RUN. DON'T WORK. DON'T THINK. NEVER LIFT A FINGER. *LET ME DO IT FOR YOU.* ALWAYS. FOREVER. FOR YOU—"

The giant voice broke into an ear-crunching sob:

"LET MAMA DO IT FOR YOU!"

"Help-p-p-p!" Irving Kittelman wailed.

"Well, there's your trouble," I said. "Sure. No question about it. Momism. Quite common among the galaxies. But it can be cured, of course."

"It can? It can?"

"Naturally. Advanced technology has done away with such minor irritations. All it takes is the right key."

"You've got it? You can help me?"

"I was just leaving."

"Wait! Hold it! We can still make a deal. Hang on. Let's talk this over."

"Well," I said. "If you'd care to come along—"

"Oh yes, I'd like that. Yes, indeed. I could look forward to something like that!"

"All right," I said. "Sure, if that's what you want."

"Oh, I do, I do. Indeed I do."

"Lean over. I'll whisper in your ear . . . There, you got that?"

Kittelman nodded.

"All right. Go ahead. Speak up now. Say it in a clear, loud voice."

Irving Kittelman turned to face the still-growing apparition. "*Mother*," he said sternly, "if you don't mind, *I'D RATHER DO IT MYSELF!*"

There was a cracking, shattering sound as if someone had dropped a carload of eggs; the beginning of a shriek.

We were back with Lund, Wanda and the leakies. Only an eye-blink had elapsed.

"A new man! A new man!" Kittelman danced. "I'm a new man! I can feel it, sense it. I'm different. I'm changed. I'm not spooked anymore. Inside me everything's different. I've been given a second chance. A new start. Inside, I've been remade."

"Well, yes, that *is* actually what's happened," I said. "More or less."

"Wow!" Lund said. "No time to waste now. Let's step on it. Just get over there, Kittelman, and get those guys back to Jewish history. Get a move on, Kittelman."

"Jewish history?" Irving Kittelman said. "What's Jewish history?"

"Oh, my god!" I groaned. "The change—it's been too much. Along with momism he's lost Jewish history, too!"

The Lund Casebook: Six

A voice said: "How do you do?"

"Greenberg!" the Tsaddik cried.

"Bossnik!"

"Quick, the Flit!" I yelled. "A devil's still loose! I thought we'd gotten rid of them."

"It's Greenberg," the Tsaddik said, "my homunculus."

"Jewish history . . . ?" Irving Kittelman said.

"Greenberg, what are you doing here?" the Tsaddik asked.

"I dropped by," Greenberg said, "to see what's cooking."

"We are," Wanda said, "if you really want to know."

"Greenberg here," the Tsaddik said, wiping his brow, "is a travel *mavin*."

"In person," Greenberg said. He put two fingers in his mouth and whistled shrilly. A bevy of little people began crawling out of the woodwork. Long beards, short, and none. Some wore black garments, others bow ties and checkered jackets. They didn't waste a second. They approached the leakies on the double. One by one the leakies began to disappear.

"Watch out," Greenberg called, "for the one who says he's Richard Nixon. He really *is* crazy. Don't worry, bossnik, we'll get them sorted in a jiffy. If not sooner."

"But how did you know where to find us?" the Tsaddik asked.

Greenberg shrugged. "I was visiting my great-grandson when right in the middle he vanished."

"Hey," Courtney said, "the pullie!"

"So he explained," Greenberg said, "when he got back. The knowledge spell told him what was going on. We sent a delegation, quick, to the galaxy under Susskind—he's the one with the long red beard who just left with King Solomon—and got everything fixed up."

"You could find the galaxy?" Courtney asked.

"Travel agents, after all," Greenberg said. "They told us at the Cosmos Corps where to find you now."

"Well, I'll be," said Courtney.

"Yeah," I said, "for a while longer, at least. And me, too; I've got to hand it to you, Tsaddik; you and your buddies really did a job. The leak's almost plugged."

"Any Tsaddik would have acted the same," the Tsaddik said.

"That goes for us homunculi, too," Greenberg said.

"So this time we're really saved?" Wanda said. "Finally, huh?"

"This is it, sweetheart," I said, "the windup. Next stop, we hit the good-time streets."

"Frankly, Lund kid, I don't know if I can stand any more hitting. Just right now."

"Don't worry, honey; I'll buy you a vitamin."

"Boy," Courtney said. "How many wonders did you pull there, Tsaddik?"

"Who keeps count?"

"At least seven, eh? At least that many, I bet. The Tsaddik of the seven wonders, eh?"

"Seven? There must have been *thousands*. Forget about this seven business."

Courtney turned to me.

"Well, there's just one thing more," he said. "The name of this world. Gloffnick. It's a terrible name. We've made so many changes here, we might at least change the name, too."

"You're right," I said. "We could change it to some basic substance."

"Like what?"

"Dirt, maybe. We could call it dirt."

"Aw, that's no good."

"No, huh?"

"Boy, that's awful."

"How about earth?"

"*Earth?* What kind of a stupid name is that?"

Glossary of Yiddish Words

ah a
ahvadeh of course
bes-medresh prayer and study house
Chelm a Polish town noted in Jewish folklore for its fools
chutspahdik impudent; impertinent
Der Forverts Yiddish daily newspaper
gevald help!
Hanukkah a Jewish holiday commemorating a victory over the Syrians and the rededication of the Temple
Hasidim pious ones—a sect of Orthodox Jewish mystics
hendim-pendim lickety-split; at full speed
heymish familiar; cozy; intimate
khokhem a smart man; a wise guy; "smarty"
krank sickness
landslite countrymen
makher an influential person; a fixer
mavin expert
mazel tov congratulations
meeskite ugliness
mekhiya (*ah*) a pleasure
mishugener (*ah*) a crazy man
narishkiyten foolish things
nebech poor thing (as in: alas, the poor thing)
nu? well?
nudnik pest
oy oh!
oysgemutshet exhausted

oysgerinen leaked out; flowed out (as in: vanished)
oy vey oh, woe; good grief
plonternish tangle
shandeh disgrace
shivah mourning
shlemiel the guy who spills the drink on the *shlimazl* (hard-lucknik)
shmutsik dirty
shtetl small town
Tsaddik saintly man
tsures woes
tumel noise; racket
umglik disaster
unshikenish affliction; nuisance
Z*ohar* book of Cabbalah: mystical commentary on the Book of Moses